Milo March is a hard-drinking, woma [ ] James-Bondian character. He always comes out [ ] combination of personality, bluff, bravado, luck, skill, experience, and intellect. He is a shrewd judge of human character, a crack shot, and a deeper character than I have found in most of the other spy/thriller novels I've read. But, above all, he is a con-man—and a very good one. It is Milo March himself who makes the series worth reading.

—Don Miller, *The Mystery Nook* fanzine 12

Steeger Books is proud to reissue twenty-three vintage novels and stories by M.E. Chaber, whose Milo March Mysteries deliver mile-a-minute action and breezily readable entertainment for thriller buffs.

Milo is an Insurance Investigator who takes on the tough cases. Organized crime, grand theft, arson, suspicious disappearances, murders, and millions and millions of dollars—whatever it is, Milo is just the man for the job. Or even the only man for it.

During World War II, Milo was assigned to the OSS and later the CIA. Now in the Army Reserves, with the rank of Major, he is recalled for special jobs behind the Iron Curtain. As an agent, he chops necks, trusses men like chickens to steal their uniforms, shoots point blank at secret police—yet shows compassion to an agent from the other side.

Whatever Milo does, he knows how to do it right. When the work is completed, he returns to his favorite things: women, booze, and good food, more or less in that order....

THE MILO MARCH MYSTERIES

Hangman's Harvest

KENDELL FOSTER CROSSEN
Writing as
M.E. CHABER

With a Foreword by
KENDRA CROSSEN BURROUGHS

STEEGER BOOKS / **2020**

PUBLISHED BY STEEGER BOOKS
Visit steegerbooks.com for more books like this.

PUBLISHING HISTORY

Hardcover
New York: Henry Holt & Co. (Holt Mystery), February 1952.
Toronto: Clarke, Irwin & Co., 1952.

Paperback
New York: Popular Library #482, as *Don't Get Caught*, 1953.
New York: Paperback Library (63-507), A Milo March Mystery, #16, January 1971. Cover by Robert McGinnis.

ISBN: 978-1-61827-495-3

For Martha

CONTENTS

FOREWORD

The Milo March Mysteries

Milo is back! As one of the children of Kendell Foster Cros-sen, I am pleased to introduce this series of twenty-two Milo March mysteries, which he wrote under the name M.E. Chaber between 1952 and 1975. The final novel in the Stee-ger Books series, *Death to the Brides,* is being published for the first time, and the last volume—#23, *The Twisted Trap*—consists of six magazine stories collected for the first time.

Milo March still has many fans, especially those who remember the Paperback Library series with the sensational Robert McGinnis cover art—more about that later. I hope Milo also attracts younger fans of vintage entertainment that is both quaint and current.

Then or now, the sources of angst are familiar—cold and hot wars, political assassination, dictators, corruption, orga-nized crime, racial conflicts, disappeared people. But it's a source of amusement to be reminded that we are in Milo's era: Ducking into drugstore booths to make calls on dial phones. Placing a long-distance call with an operator, who then listens in. Calling single women "Miss." You can pack a gun in your airline luggage, and someone comes around sell-ing cigarettes to hospital patients in bed. Milo's cases involve vast amounts of money—who wants to be a millionaire? After consulting an online inflation calculator, I remind myself that in today's money a mere million translates to over eight million green ones.

Milo may have been a gleam in his creator's eye for a dozen years since Ken Crossen began his full-time writing career in late 1939. In the 1940s he published some forty-five pulp detective and murder mystery short stories and novellas. During that time he was also writing scripts for radio mystery shows and publishing magazines and comic books—notably *The Green Lama,* based on his pulp character in *Double Detective* magazine.

Ken told an interviewer that restlessness, along with frustration with the unsuccessful publishing business, drove him to write his first novel intended for hardcover publication: "I worked out the character of Milo March, making him an insurance investigator since that was something I knew very well. I was to some degree influenced by Hemingway and Hammett, but added more of a dash of humor and more throwaway lines. Partly as a result of this, a later reviewer said that I wrote 'soft-boiled' novels."*

Crossen had worked as an insurance investigator in Cleveland—which doesn't sound terribly exciting, but it may have sparked his imagination—and his first insurance investigator story, "Homicide on the Hook" (1939), featured a detec-

---

* Steve Lewis, "Interview with Kendell Foster Crossen," *The Mystery Nook,* no. 12, June 1979. (This interview is reprinted at the back of *No Grave for March,* #2 in this Steeger Books series.) Although *Hangman's Harvest* was Crossen's first hardcover novel, he also published a couple of paperback science fiction novels in the 1950s, along with science fiction magazine stories and anthologies. He created several other detective characters besides Milo in the 1950s and '60s as well.

tive named Paul Anthony.* "The Jelly Roll Heist" was the first Milo March magazine story (published August 1952 in *Popular Detective*), but Milo's print debut was the novel *Hangman's Harvest,* first published in February 1952 in hardcover.

In *Hangman's Harvest* (1952), Milo March is a private eye employed in Denver but hired by a group of citizens in Southern California to solve a case of corruption in their city government. This story is not even about insurance investigation! But from the very beginning, it was the character of Milo that was the centerpiece. Milo in fact plays several roles in the series, including busting international crime syndicates and taking on dangerous espionage assignments as well as solving disappearances, murder mysteries, and jewel robberies.

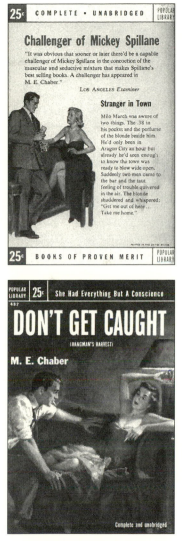

---

* *Detective Fiction Weekly,* March 23, 1940.

The second Milo March book is a Cold War spy novel set in East Germany, *No Grave for March* (1953). Milo happens to have been an OSS officer during World War II in Europe, and he is recalled to do special missions for the CIA in five of the novels and one of the short stories.*

It is not until *The Man Inside* (1954) that Milo investigates an insurance case—the theft of an immense blue diamond—in a story of psychological suspense. Though still based in Denver, Milo hops continents in pursuit of the obsessed thief, who has assumed a false identity in Spain.

He's in Ohio in #4, *As Old as Cain,* then he's a CIA operative again in *The Splintered Man* (1955), based partially on true events and featuring the use of LSD as a weapon of mind control. That story takes place in East and West Berlin and Moscow. Denver, it turns out, is the actual scene of action only in three magazine stories of 1952–1953.**

Milo moves from Denver to New York City in *A Lonely Walk* (1956), to set up his own insurance detective agency on Madison Avenue, the buckle on the Martini Belt. The sign on his office door is freshly painted and will provide the opening theme for several books: "I'm Milo March. Insurance investigator. At least that's what it says on the door to my office." There is no time for an identity crisis, as Milo is almost immediately sent to Rome on an insurance case involving murder (based on a real-life case) and government corruption.

Our hero continues to zip around the world, alighting in

---

* *No Grave for March, The Splintered Man, So Dead the Rose, Wild Midnight Falls, Death to the Brides,* and "The Red, Red Flowers."
** "The Jelly Roll Heist," "The Hot Ice Blues," and "Murder for Madame," all reprinted in #23, *The Twisted Trap: Six Milo March Stories.*

Rio de Janeiro, the Caribbean, Lisbon, Madrid, Paris, Stockholm, Hong Kong, Hanoi, and Cape Town, South Africa, with those few sneaks behind the Iron Curtain—all giving Milo a chance to show off his multilingual gifts. He speaks both Mandarin and Cantonese, and can even pass as a native speaker in German, Russian, and Spanish. His

exploits stateside take him to New Orleans, Miami, Las Vegas and Reno, San Francisco and L.A. Both small-town Ohio and Greenwich Village, New York, were homes to Ken Crossen, and his alter ego, Milo March, knows his way around them, too.

Milo March is assumed to be "tall, dark, and handsome,"* perhaps because of the famed McGinnis paperback covers, which feature a James Coburn lookalike. When asked what actor he would have liked to see portray March, Crossen named the late Humphrey Bogart.**

Robert McGinnis, in creating art for the Paperback Library reissues of 1970–1971, chose the distinctive-looking actor

---

* Robert A. Baker and Michael T. Nietzel, *Private Eyes: One Hundred and One Knights: A Survey of American Detective Fiction 1922–1984* (Bowling Green, Ohio: Bowling Green State University Popular Press, 1985), p. 151.
** Dickson Thorpe [pseudonym of Nick Carr], "Will the Real Ken Crossen Please Stand Up," *The Mystery FANcier*, vol. 1, no. 2 (March 1977), p. 6.

James Coburn as his model for Milo.* Readers have asked whether Coburn actually posed for McGinnis, or whether Coburn even knew that his image was used. The answer is revealed by Art Scott in *The Paperback Covers of Robert McGinnis:* "The reason why the fictional detective Milo March on covers of Paperback Library's 'Milo March' series looks like James Coburn is because the artist, Robert McGinnis, had some photos of Coburn he'd used previously to help him paint posters for Coburn's movies. He modeled March on these photos. To quote McGinnis, 'Coburn was easy to draw—long and lean, ideally proportioned, with a lot of character in his face.' "** In addition, Art Scott reported in *The Art of Robert E. McGinnis* that the painter anxiously expected a call from Coburn expressing his objections, but it apparently never came.

In the 1953 story "Hair the Color of Blood,"*** Milo's ID shows that at age thirty-five he is six feet tall, 185 pounds. (For the record, Bogart was five foot eight, Coburn six foot two.) Milo is not especially athletic ("I've taken a vow to never swim in anything deeper than a brandy and soda"). In *The Splintered Man* he says he "galloped past the middle thirties, getting a couple of inches thicker in the middle." When a woman says to him, "Did anyone ever tell you that you're a beautiful hunk of man?" he replies: "Usually they

---

* The Paperback Library series of twenty-five books by Kendell Foster Crossen consists of twenty Milo March novels (*Born to Be Hanged* is not included), one Kim Locke spy novel, and four novels about an insurance investigator named Brian Brett. The male characters on these book covers are not as distinctive as the Coburn lookalike who is Milo.
** Art Scott, *The Paperback Covers of Robert McGinnis* (Pond Press, 2001), p. 46.
*** *Bluebook,* July 1953.

just tell me I'm a big hunk." All the ladies who cross his path find Milo irresistible. One reviewer called this unrealistic, but that's silly. Escapist literature exists for the sake of fun, and this fills the bill.

I wonder, if books were rated like movies, how would the Milo March books fare? In general I feel that anyone who's heard of birds, bees, and bullets can enjoy these books.

Language: Men speak in "short, Hemingway-type words." (That's what Milo says instead of repeating the actual words.) Or: "He told me what I could do to myself. It wasn't very polite, so I ignored it. Never take advice from strangers." Some lines exchanged by Milo and his mobster enemies are strangely juvenile ("Go play dead"). Only once, a character exclaims, "Shit!"

Substance abuse: Steve Lewis, in reviewing a Milo March book, wrote that "if you cut out the references to drinking, the book would be at least 20 pages shorter."* Milo's drinking does seem to increase as the series advances. Social disapproval of alcoholism is obviously greater today than it was fifty-odd years ago. The recovery movement took off in the 1980s, after Ken Crossen's death. Milo says, "Many people complain that I drink a lot. I do, but I also do the things that have to be done." Throughout the series, every drink that is poured, every tinkle of ice cubes against glass, is recorded. But Milo never gets drunk—except on vodka in stories where he has assumed a Russian identity.

Violence: In several books, Milo gets a rough beating or

---

* Steve Lewis, "A PI Mystery Review: M.E. Chaber—The Flaming Man," *Mystery File,* http://mysteryfile.com/blog/?p=52513.

takes a bullet, but he himself does not have a violent nature. I like what Mike Grost writes:

Milo March stories differ radically in tone from those of Raymond Chandler. Chandler's stories are dark, and they depict a world full of evil characters. Crossen despises mobsters and crooks, but basically he likes 1950's America and the world in general. Neither he nor March seem alienated, which is the word I'd use to describe Philip Marlowe and his successors. Instead, Crossen and March preserve a sunny, good-natured attitude towards most of life. Indeed, Crossen's tone is generally comic throughout. Even his mob villains have a slightly tongue in cheek quality. Parts of the story even approach the comedy of manners, something one associates more with Golden Age sleuths than 1950's private eyes. Milo March also has a different attitude towards the men he meets than most private eyes. Usually he winds up making friends with them, and the book is full of scenes of male bonding.*

Milo uses his fists to great effect. He arms himself with one or two guns but will not kill men if shooting their kneecaps is enough. He's killed a couple of weasel-faced hoods who were pointing weapons at him, and in one case he didn't tell the cops about it.

Someone wrote that "M.E. Chaber has been called the originator of a new genre, the 'soft-boiled' suspense story, in which the emphasis is on believability of character and situation—and not a single blonde, brunette, or redhead is shot or kicked in the stomach."**

---

* http://mikegrost.com/.
** I copied those words into my notes without remembering to note the source. Shame on me!

Sex: Milo loves women, booze, and food, more or less in that order. He responds to a come-hither look and has chemistry with a certain type of woman, but he leaves the strictly-for-keeps girls alone. He expresses a preference for short, shapely brunettes, and in *The Gallows Garden* he even recites a medieval Spanish poem in praise of short women to a petite assassin who is aiming a pastel blue pistol at him. Nonetheless, his favorite

lover is a tall lady pirate from Hong Kong. Women's bodies are relished—their cleavage viewed from above, and the view from the rear as they walk away, as long as they are not wearing a girdle—but details are jauntily left to the imagination: "She wore a print dress that looked as if it had been dropped into place from a tall building as she passed beneath. In a high wind." In *So Dead the Rose,* one of my favorites, the sight of the naked breasts of an unconscious enemy agent humanizes Milo in the midst of an otherwise cold-blooded maneuver.

After a passionate kiss, Milo often picks the woman up and carries her into the bedroom—then fade to black. "We had another drink, then I took her by the hand and led her into the bedroom. We both knew about the microphone, but after a while we forgot about it."

A Milo March Mystery / 17

Nudity: In *Wanted: Dead Men* a Swedish blonde enjoys dining naked at home and urges Milo to disrobe ("You may feel silly sitting around and having a drink with your clothes off, but not as silly as you do sitting there fully dressed across from a nude broad"). Women are nude in several books ... but duh, you can't see them. The imagination gets good exercise in these fast-paced narratives.

Prejudice: There are a few outdated, derisive references to gay men ("Stay home and nurse your wrist before it becomes too limp to use a gun"). I considered editing some minor ones out but felt it wouldn't be honest. To insult a man by calling him "Percival" is more comic than offensive. Yet in *Born to Be Hanged,* Milo is a kind friend to two older men who have lived together for years; the relationship is suggestive of a marriage, a surprisingly prescient touch for a 1973 book. Milo befriends African-Americans in *A Hearse of a Different Color* (1958) and *The Flaming Man* (1969). In both novels there is a black character who hides behind stereotypical mannerisms, but Milo treats him as the intelligent human being that he is. Ken Crossen told me he created these characters deliberately, wanting to add some moral depth to these works of genre fiction.

I was slightly annoyed by the repeated Italian hood stereotype. In *A Man in the Middle* (1967), I altered the phrase "a face like a dark-complected weasel." (I left the weasel part in.) From *Six Who Ran* (1964), I deleted this sentence about a Brazilian cabbie: "His skin was so dark that I suspected it indicated an Indian ancestor somewhere." Call me P.C., but I don't know what it was supposed to imply and it seemed superfluous.

Ken Crossen remained with the same publishing company for all of the published Milo March books,* and I imagined his editors would keep track of previous books in the series, taking note of characters who appeared in more than one book and ensuring consistency of details. To my disappointment, this was not the case, and I decided to copyedit all of the books, since I am a professional book editor. I also added some footnotes, chiefly about dated references and verse in foreign languages. It's a nerdy touch that may be helpful to some readers.

My editing rarely required changes to the actual wording and was mostly concerned with consistency of style. However, in several books I did a bit more than that. For example, in *Born to Be Hanged,* the final book published in Crossen's lifetime—which is #21 in the series—a character from #18 is mentioned. He is called Gino Mancetti in #21, and it is noted that he was involved in a prior case, which is very clearly the one from #18, *The Flaming Man.* But in #18, the character's name is Gino Benetto.

If only it were just a matter of changing "Mancetti" to "Benetto." The problem is that Milo shot Gino Benetto in both knees in #18. A cop remarked that Benetto would probably never walk again. Yet in #21, there is no sign of Mancetti's having any infirmity, and the fact that Milo ever shot him is not mentioned when they meet.

So I changed "Gino Mancetti" in #21 to "Dino Mancetti," to make him different from "Gino Benetto" in #18. And I made it less specific about where Milo knows him from.

---

* His publisher went through various incarnations as Henry Holt & Co., Rinehart & Co., and Holt, Rinehart & Winston.

Finally, in the last novel, #22, *Death to the Brides,* Crossen inserted a character from another series, Major Kim Locke of the CIA, briefly into the plot. Kim is lending his military service dog, Dante, to Milo for a mission in Vietnam. I had to change the breed of the dog, as I explain in the afterword to that book. If this were the same Dante that had been Major Locke's dog in 1953, that heroic canine would have gone to his reward by 1975. The other problem is that Dante was a Hungarian Puli (a breed that lives to about age sixteen), which has fur in long dreds. The breed is too heavy and hairy to be carried through the Vietnamese jungle, which is what Milo does with Dante in #22.

After conferring with the science fiction author Richard Lupoff, who helped me edit *Death to the Brides,* I changed the dog to a miniature pinscher, named Dante after his predecessor. (I learned that the US military does utilize miniature breeds for certain missions.) Although Ken Crossen had several favorite poets, I didn't want to take the liberty of renaming Dante. (Ken really liked Robert Service, the Bard of the Yukon, but I couldn't name a service dog Service.)

In real life, Ken Crossen named his own dog Milo.

Kendra Crossen Burroughs

PROLOGUE

Pallida Mors aequo pulsat pede ... *

Cities are like women. Some are softly rounded and seductive. Some are brazen, with scarlet slashes across their faces. There are cities that are noisy and nagging, and cities that cling to the strong arm. There are cities which are always just out of reach, with hard, defiant little haunches moving with provocation beneath the surface.

Aragon City is like a successful call girl in church on Sunday. She sits primly on the coast of California with her back to the Pacific. To her north is Santa Monica; to her south, Ocean Park. But directly in front of her is Los Angeles, sprawling around Hollywood as though trying to hide it. Los Angeles, a tumorous growth of flat, ugly buildings hiding beneath layers of smog. And within the growth, Hollywood, the city without a charter and with no city limits; Hollywood, with its movie stars and tabernacles, Dianetics and Vedanta, sewing circles and call houses—where pimps represent actors and directors and writers as well as ladies of the evening.

And Aragon City, her fresh and innocent air a gift from the

---

* The first five words of a line from the *Odes* of Horace: "Pale Death, with impartial step, knocks at the cottages of the poor and the palaces of kings." (All footnotes were added by the editor.)

Pacific, sits on the edge of her seat and waits for the services to be over.

It was night in Aragon City and the wind from the ocean was cool. Down near the boardwalk old men sat outside, letting the cold remind them of the east or the west or the north. Above their heads the palm trees waved to each other.

On Vallejo Street, a pale green Cadillac swept into the curb and stopped. The sleek-looking man walked into the apartment house and returned in a few minutes.

"A dozen sticks," he said to the girl as he slid in behind the wheel. "We're riding high tonight, baby."

Two dozen men and women crouched over a green baize table in a club on the ocean front. Their eyes were feverish as they watched the spinning wheel. Their breathing matched the clacking rhythm of the ball.

A hopped-up Ford squealed to a stop in front of a liquor store on Poinsettia. A boy went in and bought six bottles of a famous soft drink.

"There's a bottle apiece and two extra for you girls," he said as he came back.

Across the street from the Pollux Club a nervous man chewed on his unlighted cigarette and rubbed his cheek against the stock of a rifle. He watched the door of the club, peering beneath the shadow signboard.

The man who came in on the airliner at the International Airport was early. But he wanted to arrive before he was expected; to wander around and feel the city before it knew he was there. He checked his bags at the airport and took a cab to Aragon City.

He went from bar to bar, from club to club. In each he had one drink. Brandy and water. He drank slowly, watching the faces around him, listening to conversations which had no meaning. He looked for nothing special, but collected the faces and the sounds on his nerve ends.

By midnight the only evidence of the brandies was the warmth under his belt. And he knew Aragon City for what she was. He could feel her lack of roots, the violence that bubbled just beneath the surface. He could feel something within him answering the violence.

He walked into a small, dimly lit club on Portola. He sensed a difference as he walked to the bar. Even before he looked around he knew what he'd see. Everyone there was better dressed than in the bars he'd visited earlier—sleeker, more enameled. The men's coats were more padded in the shoulders and some were tailored to hide bulges under the arms or in the pockets. Here and there he could spot the ones who came to see, to rub shoulders.

He ordered his drink and became aware of the woman who sat next to him at the bar. Her perfume reached out to tug at his senses. He took a quick look. Evening dress. Plunging neckline. Mink stole. Careful blond hair. Her face was familiar. He searched his memory and found the face staring out from a movie screen. He turned back to his drink.

Later he knew she was examining him. He kept his eyes on his drink, letting her take her time. He didn't know if he was interested, but if it turned out that he was, he liked women to know what they wanted.

He saw two men in the mirror. One was entering and one

was leaving. For a minute they stopped and stared at each other. Nothing was said, but you could feel the tightening all over the room. Low-voiced conversations fell off. The room waited, and then the two men nodded to each other and passed.

He felt the shudder that moved over the woman. In surprise, he looked at her. She stared back at him. There was excitement in her eyes. And something else.

It was after one when he left the club with her. She handed him her car keys and pointed out the convertible. It was starting to rain so he put the top up. In the car she leaned against his shoulder, occasionally calling out directions in a sleepy voice.

It was a small estate in the residential section of Aragon City. There was an electronic beam and the heavy wrought-iron gates automatically swung open and then closed after the car. They left the car beneath the car porch. He unlocked the door with her key and followed her in.

In the modern living room, she tossed her handbag on a chair and turned to him, holding her arms out in drunken gravity.

"Put me to bed," she said simply. She swayed toward him.

He picked up her limp form and carried her out into the foyer. After a couple of wrong guesses, he found the bedroom. He paused uncertainly, then deposited her on the bed. She sagged back on the cover, her eyes closed.

He dropped to one knee and removed her shoes. He ran his hands up along her silkened legs, beneath the evening gown. There was warm flesh against his fingers as he fumbled with the garter snaps, then he peeled off the skeins of silk. Her body was limp as he lifted it to pull the evening dress over her head. Beneath the dress, she wore only the gossamer garter belt.

He hung the dress in her closet, put the shoes on a shoe rack. The stockings and garter belt he tossed over the back of a chair. He turned to look at her.

He hadn't switched on a light in the bedroom, and the glow of a distant street lamp slanted through the open Venetian blinds to paint her body with ivory and shadows. He reached down to touch one of her firm breasts, and the nipple nestled against the palm of her hand. He let his breath out slowly and his gaze stroked over the rest of her body. It was a well-cared-for body, a delicate hint of curve between navel and cleft, the legs strong and shapely.

He pulled the covers down beneath her so that she rested on the sheets. She still seemed submerged in a drunken sleep, but he was suddenly aware that her breathing was too deep and rapid. A panel of light was across her face and he saw the quiver of a curled eyelash against her cheek.

Anger stirred within him as he stood up. A moment later, savagely, he turned back toward her.

Outside, the tempo of the storm picked up with a sullen fury. The wind swooped down the street, clattering over garbage can lids, snatching up bits of paper and dispatching them into nowhere; it forced its way up the narrow alleys, thrusting its unappeased strength against the very windows, raged through the city. And then the rains came spurting from the skies. Lightning split the clouds and thunder shook the ground.

Here and there a sleeper stirred uneasily, but the honest citizens of Aragon City slept on, unaware that the storm was ravishing their city.

ONE

I was due in Aragon City at eight that night. On Flight 324 from Denver. I had another brandy and water in a bar on Third Street and got into a cab. It was a quarter to eight when I got to the International Airport.

The girl at the desk said that Flight 324 was on time. I lit a cigarette and took a quick look around the waiting room. There were a lot of people but nobody who looked like they belonged on a committee. Then the public address system came to life and I knew why.

"Mr. Milo March, there is a telephone call for you in booth three next to the United Airlines counter."

I grinned and ducked out, taking the underground passage to the gates. The phone call meant that they hadn't bothered to ask if the plane was in or that they suspected I was there early. Not that it made any difference. But I was still going to make it look like I came in on the right flight.

After a while the big transport lumbered off the strip and wheeled around with one wing pointing at the gates. When the passengers came off, I walked along with them into the waiting room. Just to make it artistic, I looked around as if I were expecting someone to meet me. It was wasted, but it made me feel good.

I didn't have to wait long. "Mr. Milo March," the girl's voice said over the loudspeaker, "there is a telephone call for you in booth three next to the United Airlines counter."

I walked over to the booth and took the receiver from the hook. "Milo March," I said.

"Just a minute, sir," the operator said. I waited.

"Milo March?" a new voice asked. It was a man with a salad voice. Crisp.

"Yeah," I said and waited some more.

"This is Willis—Chairman of the committee. Did you just get in?"

"Isn't this when I was due?" I countered. I grinned, remembering the twenty-four hours I'd already spent in Aragon City.

"Of course, of course," he said hastily. "We were going to meet you, March, but thought better of it. Will you come straight here? The address is three-two-two Loma Vista Boulevard. The third floor."

"Okay," I said, and hung up. I reclaimed the stuff I'd checked the night before and went out and got a cab. I gave the driver the address and leaned back in the seat.

I already had an idea what it was going to be like. You get feelings like that some days. This was going to be a job that could be summed up with one word. Messy.

Two weeks before this Willis had gotten in touch with me by long-distance phone. First he'd told me who he was. Linn Willis. Sometimes consulting engineer to the Air Force. Owner of the Willis Aircraft Corporation in Aragon City, California. Owner of the *Aragon City News.* A big shot. Then he added that he was Chairman of the Aragon City Civic Betterment Committee. I could already smell the next step.

Aragon City was steeped in crime—that was his word, steeped—and they wanted a competent investigator to prepare a report for the Civic Betterment Committee. I had been highly recommended to the committee. They wanted to hire me.

I said no. I said that I already had a job, I liked the job, I was eating regularly, and I didn't give a damn if the hoods took over Aragon City. He said he hoped I'd think it over and then hung up.

The next night he called again. He said that he'd arranged with my present employer for me to have a leave of absence. He said that money was no object. I still didn't like playing, so he repeated the business about thinking it over and hung up again. The next morning, when I got to the office, he was on the phone again. This time it was a three-way conversation. Willis, my boss, and me. Somehow or other, I got the idea that I had a leave of absence whether I wanted it or not and that I'd better at least go out and talk it over with Willis and his committee. He was an even bigger man that I'd thought.

I bought two plane tickets to Los Angeles and used the first one. The two tickets you could mark down to habit, but the early arrival was so I could get in one look at the town before anyone knew I was there. I got the look.

The cab pulled up in front of the building on Loma Vista Boulevard. I thought of having him wait, but then I changed my mind. I paid the driver and lugged my two suitcases into the building with me.

If the reception room on the third floor was any indication, the Civic Betterment Committee couldn't do much better by itself. The rugs were soft and the lights were softer. The furniture was so modem you began to feel old-fashioned the minute you looked at it. Then you looked at the receptionist and forgot the place even had furniture. She had red hair and it looked real. Her face must have been worth a bonus every month from her employer just to keep her from taking a screen test. And I was willing to bet that she was real below the shoulders too. They don't make the phony ones that good. The rest of her was hidden by the desk, but you could sense that every curve was there.

She was giving me a fast inventory too, and when her eyes met mine I could tell that she knew what I was going to say. So I didn't say it.

"Some joint you got here," I said casually, with a nod of my head just to show that I knew there was furniture there.

"Joint?" she said. Her eyebrows went up a little, which was a score on my side. I dropped my suitcases to the floor.

"Yeah." I took another look around the room and then brought my gaze back where it belonged. "This is the hotel, isn't it?"

"Hotel?" she repeated. She was really getting off balance. "Whatever made you think it was a hotel?"

"Some fellow down on the street," I said.

She wasn't sure of herself anymore, but she was still trying to look inside my head. "You're kidding me, aren't you?" she asked.

I shook my head. Then I let my eyes open wide in surprise. "You don't mean this is a—" I broke off and looked her over carefully. "No! I don't believe it."

She got what I meant. Her head came up and you could see the ice beginning to form in her throat. "This," she said coldly, "is the Aragon City Civic Betterment Committee."

"Honey, they *couldn't* do better than you," I said. I grinned at her. "If this isn't a hotel, maybe they've got some rooms for rent where you live."

She laughed. It was a nice laugh. While I was enjoying it, I moved over and sat on the edge of her desk. I looked down at her. I'd been right. They were real.

"What is this?" she said. "Or, rather, who are you?"

"This," I said in my best voice, "is the Aragon City Civic Betterment Committee. Remember? And I'm the guy who came in wanting to know if it was a hotel. Now, shall we go on from there?"

She laughed again and moved her chair. It spoiled the range, so I went back to looking at her face.

The door in back of her opened and we both looked up. The man in the doorway was maybe fifty and looked like he had a million for every year of it. He noticed right away where I was sitting, and he tried to ignore it at the same time he registered disapproval. It was quite a feat and he almost brought it off.

"Miss Carr," he said, in the same lettuce voice I'd heard on the phone, "you *will* show Mr. March in the minute he arrives?"

Her uncertainty came back and she looked at me. But when I didn't say anything she turned back to him. "Of course, Mr. Willis," she said. She took another fast look at me. It was obvious that she felt she had to make some explanation about me.

It was equally obvious that he was going to wait for it. "This gentleman—" she began.

"Hold it, honey," I said. I slid off the desk and waited until he looked at me too. "I'm Milo March. I was just getting ready to tell Miss Carr who I was when you came in."

"Oh, was that what you were doing," he said. It was an observation, not a question. And I noticed that the crispness didn't altogether disguise a nasty note when he felt like using it. "Well, we're waiting for you, March."

"I know," I said. We played the waiting game again, then he turned and led the way into the next room. I winked at the receptionist and followed.

There were six other people seated around a big table in the room. It looked like a conference. But I saw one of them before any of the others. She was wearing a different perfume today. And a tailored suit instead of an evening dress. But it was the same careful blond hair.

Willis had already paused beside her chair. "Mr. March, Miss Vega Russell," he said. "Miss Russell is very civic-minded, but she is perhaps better known as a star of the screen."

"How do you do, Mr. March," she said in a starched voice. It took me a minute to place the voice. It was from her last picture.

"I've seen Miss Russell before," I said, not bothering to mention that it had been the night before. But I was thinking about it. Long ago I'd come to the conclusion that there are no accidents—that's why I never have any.

But Willis was leading me along to the next person. Another

woman. This one was old. Very old, by the testimony of the wrinkles on her face. But her eyes were young and she sat more erect than anyone in the room. She wore a high-collared black silk dress. I hadn't seen one like it since the last time I saw a picture of Queen Victoria.

"And this is Miss Elizabeth Saxon," Willis was saying. "She is Aragon City's oldest citizen and has long taken a most active interest in civic affairs." Something about his voice made me think that Linn Willis didn't much like Miss Saxon.

She looked at me with those young-old eyes and snorted. "Well," she said, "at least you look relatively honest. I suppose one can't ask for more."

I decided that Miss Saxon and I would get along.

Willis took me around the table, introducing me to the others. George Stern. A lawyer. Middle-aged and fat. Donald Reid. A banker. He shook hands as if he suspected you wouldn't give his hand back. Sherman Marshall. Commissioner of Parks for Aragon City. A man who was always looking for votes. Dr. David Jilton. Young but with a permanent bedside manner. And if you could believe Willis, all of them were so civic-minded they were about to burst with it.

When I'd been introduced, had my hand pumped, and been inspected, mostly with disapproval, Willis motioned me to a chair at one end of the table and he went to the other end. Then we all sat around the table looking important.

"We," Linn Willis finally said, "are pretty much in agreement that you're the man we want, March, and—"

"Just a minute," I said. "You may be in agreement, but I'm not. I came out here because there wasn't much else I could do about that, but there are a couple of things which have to be cleared up before I agree to work for you."

"Oh," Willis said. He was a great man with the Oh. "What is it you wish to know?"

"First, why do you want to hire me?"

"I thought I explained that we want you to conduct an investigation and give us a report on the crime situation in Aragon City."

"Yeah, but *why?* Why do you want such a report?"

"We have reason to believe," Willis said, still sounding like he was giving a fiscal report to his stockholders, "that there is considerable crime in Aragon City. That is, undetected crime. We have been given to understand that there is large-scale gambling going on, considerable traffic in drugs, and that the morals of our city are being endangered by the presence of a great many—ah—houses of ill fame."

I looked at the man in amazement. I hadn't heard anyone talk like that since I was a kid. There was a minister in our town who used to preach against the houses of ill fame, and it was six months before anyone realized he was talking about the two tramps who lived down by the railroad yards and took care of the quarry workers every Saturday night.

"Young man," Miss Saxon said in her raspish voice, "he's talking about whores."

Everybody got a little pink except Vega Russell, Miss Saxon, and me. And I loved the old lady. "I kind of thought so," I said gravely, "but I was waiting for him to stop trying to clean it up. I guess he means the town is full of sausage factories."

This was a new one on them, and everyone tried to look ignorant except Miss Saxon. She beamed at me.

"We are told," Linn Willis said, and I noticed that he was being careful to point out that his information hadn't been obtained directly, "that Aragon City is full of prostitutes."

"Whores," the old lady muttered, but loud enough for everyone to hear. Linn Willis glared at her.

I grinned at everybody. "Okay," I said, "so your city is overrun with gamblers, drug peddlers, and whores. I still want to know why you want to hire me."

"What do you mean?"

"It's simple," I said. "The kind of crime you're talking about is big-league stuff. It's organized all over the country. Whatever you've got here is bankrolled by the boys in Chicago or New York, and they're taking their cut. It's not much of a secret that the Aragon City end is being run by two men. Jan Lomer and Johnny Doll.* Lomer is the brains and Doll's the muscle. Everybody knows this from the FBI on down, but you don't see either of them going to jail, and it's doubtful if they will. The FBI, the Treasury boys, and the Senate Crime Committee have all gone over these boys with fine-tooth combs. And got nothing. So if you're hiring me to write up a report saying that Jan Lomer and Johnny Doll head up the crime in this section, you're throwing your dough away. I just gave you that report for nothing. On the other hand, if you expect me to hand you evidence that will put Lomer and Doll in jail, you've got rocks in your head. I couldn't find it where better men have failed, and I like living too much to try."

---

* This seems like a play on Johnny Dollar, the private eye in a 1940s radio show.

Linn Willis started to say something, but I held up my hand to head him off. I took a deep breath and started again.

"The other angle," I said, "is that maybe you want me to buck your city police force and local politics. If this is it, I want to know more about where I stand. It doesn't take a genius to guess that somebody in the city is crooked, and probably a lot of them."

"Where did you get that idea?" Willis asked quickly.

"I said you don't have to be a genius. Half of the people in this town are sure that the whole political setup is getting paid off. You ought to get out and listen to the people who don't travel in your circles. When you add what they're saying to the fact that there are a lot of hoods in town who look fat and unafraid, and the existence of a Civic Betterment Committee, you get political graft."

Everybody but Vega Russell looked surprised. They all thought I had arrived only that night and come straight to their office, so they couldn't figure out how I knew what the man in the street was saying. I didn't bother to explain it.

"I resent that, young man," one of the men said. I remembered that he was the one who was introduced as the Commissioner of Parks. "I have been in politics for—"

"Oh, shut up, Sherman," Miss Saxon said. "Do you want a chance to become mayor or don't you?"

Sherman Marshall gulped and sank back in his seat. Miss Saxon looked at me and smiled dryly. "Sherman is an awful idiot," she said, "but he *is* honest." She turned back to the others. "The young man is right. He's got to be told exactly where we stand."

"I agree," Linn Willis said, to my surprise. He looked around the table at the others, and one by one they nodded. He turned back to me. When he spoke, he was using his chairman-of-the-board voice again.

"We are, of course, aware of the existence of Lomer and Doll. We trust that eventually something can be done about them. But, in the meantime, we are quite certain that they do have connections with certain individuals in the present administration. We won't name whom we suspect at this point; we may be wrong in the actual individuals, but it makes little difference. If such connections do exist, the administration is responsible. We want you to find evidence of such connections between Aragon City officials and Lomer and Doll, or their representatives. On the basis of such evidence, we will launch a reform ticket in the next election."

"If I find the connection," I said, "it'll probably lead no farther than an errand boy for Lomer and Doll. You know that, don't you?"

"On that end, we'll take what we can get," Willis said. "Chiefly, we want from you proof concerning the persons in the administration of Aragon City who are giving protection to these crimes. We'd like it if you'd get us some real evidence against Lomer and Doll, but if you can't, then we'll find ways of making things difficult for them after the reform group is in."

"Okay, so far," I said. "But there are a couple of other things. First, my fee. It will be a minimum of five thousand—win, lose, or draw. Ten thousand if I hand you everything you want."

Willis looked around the table again, but I noticed his gaze stayed longest on the old lady. And when she nodded, he turned back to me.

"We are prepared to pay that fee," he said.

"Plus expenses," I said.

"We expected to pay your expenses," he said stiffly.

"One more thing," I said. "It has to be understood that I am strictly on my own. Until my report is ready, I take no orders from any of you, nor do I report anything to you."

This time he didn't look around the table, but he did hesitate.

"It's that way," I said, "or you can get yourself another boy."

"Very well," he said finally. "It seems to me that this is most unorthodox, but you *are* highly recommended. We agree."

"Then you've hired yourself a boy. Anything else you want to give me?"

"No more information at this time," Willis said. "We will all provide you with any information you want when we can. But note that I say *information*. We will not pass along any of our guesses."

"I like it that way."

"We have made certain arrangements for you," Willis continued. He drew two keys from his pocket and placed them on the table. Then from another pocket he drew three papers and added them to the keys. "We have arranged an apartment for you. It's at Sixty-two Miramar Terrace. I—ah—happen to own the building myself, so no one except this Committee knows that it has been turned over to you. There is a phone in the apartment with an unlisted number. Only this Committee knows the number."

A real babe in the woods, I thought. He was making it sound like cops-and-robbers stuff. But I figured they were all enjoying themselves so much, I wouldn't spoil it. But I knew that within about twenty-four hours I'd be about as secret as the weather reports.

"We are also providing a car for you," Willis continued. "You will find it parked downstairs. It's a black Cadillac, license number 8T6860. It's registered in your name. And here is a California driver's license in your name."

He paused for me to be impressed. I grinned.

"Then we thought it best for you to have some authority. The District Attorney, Martin Yale, is with us, so we've arranged for you to be on his staff of investigators. Here, also, is a gun permit."

They were all beaming at me, so I didn't have the heart to make the crack I wanted to. Besides, they might have gone right out and enrolled me in the Boy Scouts.

"Okay," I said. "What else?"

"That is all," he said. "After tonight you're on your own. And I'd like to wish you good luck."

So I went through the hand-shaking business again. I don't know what caused it, but this time Vega Russell was getting that look in her eyes again. But I played it like it was written for Joseph Breen's office. Then I scooped up the keys and the papers and went through the door.

The redhead looked up as I came out.

"That was a mean trick," she said, but she didn't mean it.

"Sorry, honey," I said. "It was the bright lights. They brought out my acting blood."

"Speaking of acting," she came back, "what did you think of the glamour member of our committee?" It wasn't just idle curiosity. She knew where the competition was.

"A dish," I said. I held it a minute while I checked up. "But take you, now—you're the whole set. By the way ..."

"Yes?"

"I guess I won't be needing to rent that room now. They've given me an apartment. So far I have only one key to it, but I could get a duplicate made ..."

A buzzer rang and she jumped at the out. But not too fast.

"Excuse me," she said. "Mr. Willis wants me."

"I don't blame him a bit, honey," I said. I stood and watched her as she went into the conference room. She had a nice walk—especially in the hips.

I picked up my suitcases and went downstairs. I found the Cadillac without any trouble. I looked at it and grinned. They were the kind of people who probably had never gotten around to noticing that some people didn't drive Cadillacs. Especially D.A.'s investigators. Not the honest ones.

But I had no objection to letting some of their luxury rub off. I got in the Cadillac and drove off. It went away from there with a smooth surge that reminded me of the redhead.

I stopped in a gas station and got the directions to Miramar Terrace. It was about a twenty-minute drive. The apartment house was up in a fairly good residential section, on high enough ground so you could see the ocean. I stood outside and looked. The moon was cutting a path across the water and there was a breeze from the ocean that was clean and fresh. I figured it would be the last thing that was clean and fresh that I'd come across for several days, so I took my fill of it.

Then I went inside. According to the mailboxes, there were four apartments in the building and I was in number three. I walked up the stairs and slipped the key in the lock. The door opened and I stepped inside, closing the door behind me. I fumbled around the wall, feeling for a light button.

It was dark in the apartment. There were Venetian blinds over the window and they were closed so that only a dim glow came through from the streetlights. There was a faint odor of perfume in the apartment. There was musk in it, so my guess was that the previous occupant had been young and available.

I found the light switch and flicked it, thinking that it would be nice if somebody had made a mistake and left the girl in the apartment.

They had.

The studio bed in the living room was made up. Clean sheets and everything. The sheets weren't even mussed because the girl was lying on top of the covers. On her back, with her hands clasped under her head. Her hair was the color of corn silk. It drifted around on the pillow, framing a face that was as beautiful as anything you'll ever see on a bill-board. In these days of movies, television, and glamour ads, you begin to suspect beauty like that. But she had very little makeup on and there was nothing to keep me from seeing that she was a natural blonde.

Her clothes were all draped over the nearest chair. Neat. But not half as neat as the figure draped on the bed, so I went back to looking at it. There wasn't a line or a curve out of place. A symphony in flesh. By the time I got around to looking at her face again, she was smiling.

"Any complaints?" she asked. Her voice was soft, with the sort of undertones that scrape along your spine like silk.

"The complaint department just went out of business," I said. I glanced at the key in my hand and then looked up again. At her face. "I must have gotten in the wrong apartment," I said. I didn't bear down too hard on the "wrong."

"Not if you're Milo March."

"I'm Milo March," I admitted.

"Then you're in the right apartment," she said. She rolled over on her side, facing me. "I'm Mickie Gill. Hello."

"Hello," I said uncertainly. A silent bell was trying to ring in the back of my head.

Her eyebrows went up. "You're a funny guy," she said.

"I am?" I asked automatically. I was thinking and listening to that silent bell even though I didn't want to.

"Your eyes say I'm welcome, but your voice doesn't sound too sure." She slid from the bed in one graceful movement and stood up. She went up on her toes and twisted her body into profile. It was almost enough to put the warning bell out of order. "Maybe *I'm* in the wrong apartment," she said, giving me an amused glance. She didn't mean it any more than I had.

"You're in the right apartment," I said, "but maybe it's the wrong time. Will it do any good to ask who sent you?"

She looked surprised. "Why not?" she said. She sat on the bed. "Give me a cigarette."

I walked across the room and handed her a cigarette. Then I held my lighter for her. My hand didn't shake much.

"Okay, who sent you?" I asked. I stepped back. There was no point to stacking the cards against myself.

"Polly East," she said. She gave me another smile. "It's on the house—if that's what's worrying you."

I didn't know the name of Polly East, but I didn't have to after her last sentence. Mickie Gill was a professional. I took another look at her, but she looked just as good.

"On the house, huh?" I said. "That must make this an honor. You look as if you came off the high-priced shelf."

"High enough," she said, shrugging her shoulders. There was a new expression in her eyes. "You sound like you were cooling off. Maybe you thought I was a nice neighborly girl with an itch and that was okay, but now it's different. Is that how it is?"

"You got me all wrong, Mickie," I said. "I got nothing against hothouses. This is something different."

"How different?"

"Maybe I don't like presents," I said. "Let's put it that way. You come back some other night and I'll pay my own freight. Right now, honey, there's only one thing I want more than you—and that's to have you dressed and out of here in about three minutes. Can you do that and still be friends?"

She gave me a long look. Whatever was up, she didn't know she was part of it and somehow that made me feel better. She must have seen what I was feeling, for she got up from the bed and went to her clothes.

"A frame?" she asked quietly. But she was already dressing.

"I think so," I said. "I'm sorry, Mickie," I added.

"So am I," she said. "I don't like things like that. I'm going to find out ..."

She was dressing in a hurry, but even so she was graceful. If I hadn't been thinking about other things, I would have enjoyed watching her dress. And that was a switch.

I didn't have a watch on her, but I think she made it in three minutes, including checking her face and hair. She made a last smoothing gesture to her dress and nodded. I opened the door and looked out. It was clear and I held the door open.

"You come back, Mickie," I said, "and if you just want to sit around and talk—okay. In fact, I'd like that too." I decided not to mention money for talking. I could see she was thinking and it was better to make it friendly.

"We'll see," she said. "Good luck, Milo." She was gone.

I had regrets, but I didn't pamper them. I closed the door and went through the apartment on the run. I checked closets, under the bed and chairs, the bathroom, the kitchen, and even the garbage can. There was nothing around that shouldn't have been.

Then I went back to the kitchen. When I'd gone through it, I'd noticed that it was well furnished with food and some bottles. One of the bottles was brandy. I opened it, put some water in a glass, and carried the bottle into the other room. I threw my coat over the chair, splashed some brandy into the glass, and set the bottle on the floor. I lit a cigarette. Then I stretched out on the bed and tried to look like a tired businessman relaxing after a hard day.

"March," I said to myself, "two will get you twenty that the cops will be here within fifteen minutes."

They were there in ten.

The knock on the door wasn't loud, but there was a firmness about it. You can always recognize a cop's knock. They all knock as if there was something illegal about a door being closed.

"Come in," I said. I'd left the door unlocked the last time I'd closed it.

The door opened and two guys walked in. They were in plainclothes. One of them was a little paunchy around the middle and he had the tired eyes of a man who's been tramping around knocking on doors too long. He even walked flat-footed. The other one was tall and skinny. And bright-eyed. He was the hungry one. But the first one was the one to watch. You could tell by looking at him that he believed in a strong arm and to hell with the questions.

"Hi," I said, waving the glass in their direction. "What can I do for you?"

"Where is she?" It was the skinny guy, just like I'd expected. The other one was looking around with his tired eyes.

"Who?" I asked innocently.

They didn't bother to answer. The paunchy guy was already walking flatfootedly into the next room. The skinny guy stayed to watch me.

"Who're you looking for?" I repeated.

"The dame," he said.

"What dame?"

He looked at me and grinned, but it didn't mean anything except that his lips moved.

"Look," I said, sitting up, "if you're some guy out looking for his wife, or something like that, I'm no wife collector."

The paunchy guy came back. He looked disappointed. He shook his head at his partner.

"What did you do with her?" the skinny guy wanted to know.

"I don't know what you're talking about," I said. I set the glass on the floor. It was time to be indignant. "Now, what the hell's this all about? You got no right to come in like this. I got a notion to call the cops."

"All you have to do is whisper," the skinny guy said. He gave me that grin again. His hand came out of his pocket and he flipped his palm toward me. The badge was there. "Headquarters."

"Him, too?" I asked, indicating the other.

"Sure. Show the man your badge, Harry."

The paunchy one showed me his badge like he was afraid I'd steal some of the nickel off it.

The skinny cop was sniffing the air. "She's been here," he said to the other guy. "Maybe he's part rabbit … But you can still smell the perfume. What about that, March?"

He knew my name and everything.

"The perfume," I said. "Oh, I always dab a little behind my ears when I come home. I never know when some of you boys will drop in."

The skinny one looked at me brightly. "A smart one," he said. "You notice, Harry, how he suddenly got smart with the answers."

"Yeah." His voice was as tired as his eyes.

"Okay, so you're cops," I said. "Have you got names or only badges?"

"I'm Grant," the skinny one said. He jerked a thumb at the other cop. "He's Fleming. Now, you want to tell us about the dame?"

"You got a fixation or something?" I said. "If you're so hard up, I could maybe send you to a good address. Polly East's."

Fleming had been looking at me all the time. Now he looked at Grant. "Being he's new in town," he said in that tired voice, "he could maybe not be familiar with the stairs and fall down them." He was flexing the fingers of his right hand.

Grant shook his head, but for a minute his eyes were brighter. "Not yet, Harry," he said. He continued looking at me. "We got a tip," he said, "that you had a dame up here. It smells like the tip was right, only we got here too late."

"So sorry you had the trip for nothing," I said. "Close the door as you leave." I picked up the glass and stretched out again.

The two of them stared at me. "No, Harry," Grant said, like he was a mind reader. "We're going, March. But we don't like some strangers in town. We'll be seeing you."

"Yeah," Harry Fleming said.

They went out and closed the door. Hard.

I drank the brandy and needed it. I wasn't kidding myself about those two. It was written all over them.

I was on my second drink when the phone rang. I picked it up.

"Hello," I said.

"Hello, darling," the voice said. It was a woman's voice, but deep. It sounded like a lot of Canadian Club. "This is Polly East."

"Hi, Polly," I said. And waited.

"I sent a girl out to see you tonight," she said. "Mickie Gill. Did she get there?"

"Came and gone," I said. "How'd you know she was my type?"

She chuckled like she was proud of herself. "That took a little work, but I did it. You know Babe Dale?"

I knew Babe Dale. She was the fanciest madam in Denver. I said I knew her.

"Well," said Polly, "I called Babe and asked her what kind of girls you liked. She told me and I sent Mickie. How'd you like her?"

"I liked Mickie all right," I said, "even though she wasn't here more than a few minutes after I arrived. But I didn't care much for the two cops who came ten minutes later. You send them, too?"

There was a long silence. "Are you kidding me, darling?" the woman asked.

"About liking them? Not at all. They smelled like cops."

"I knew nothing about cops," she said, and her voice was hard. "I don't play like that, Milo. I'll look into it and maybe I can square it. I'll let you know."

She hung up. I grinned at the phone and put the receiver back.

Three or four brandies later, I went to bed. Some of Mickie's perfume was still clinging to the pillow, and that didn't make it any easier to fall to sleep. So I started thinking about the redhead in the reception room of the Civic Betterment Committee, and that made it even harder to go to sleep.

I thought about the Committee and grinned to myself. They had made such a big thing about being secretive. Nobody knew the apartment, an unlisted phone number, and all that. So before I'd been in the apartment an hour, I'd been visited by a fancy call girl and two tough cops, and had a phone call from Aragon City's leading madam. Some secret.

TWO

It was a nice morning. The sun was shining, in oblique bars, through the blinds. Outside I could hear the wind running its fingers through the tops of the palm trees. I had a cigarette in bed and let the new day creep up on me. The smell of Mickie Gill's perfume was finally gone from the pillow.

After a while I got up and went into the bathroom. I took a shower and shaved. Then I got dressed and went into the kitchen. I had to say one thing for the Committee—they knew how to stock a kitchen even if they weren't so good at keeping a secret. I had orange juice, bacon and eggs, and coffee. Just on the chance that it might be a rough day, I laced the coffee with a little brandy.

It was almost ten when I finished my breakfast. I figured it was still too early for callers, so I'd have time for one more personal thing. I dialed the number of the Aragon City Civic Betterment Committee.

"Good morning," a girl's voice answered. It was the redhead. Even bad phone service couldn't disguise the silk in her voice.

"Miss Carr?" I said as formally as I could.

"This is Miss Carr speaking."

"Miss Carr, I represent the Frammis Lineage Corporation,"*
I said, trying to put a little lettuce in my voice so it would
sound as stuffy as Linn Willis's. "We are making up a directory of all the Carrs in California. Would you mind telling me
your first name?"

There was a pause and then she laughed. It was such a nice
laugh that it brought up memories of the way her hips moved
when she walked. "Good morning, Mr. March," she said.

"*My* first name is Milo," I said. I liked her answer. I'd
wondered how quick she was on the uptake. Sometimes
those high-polished jobs don't have anything but enamel
above the bustline.

She laughed again. "It's Betty," she said. "Did you want to
speak to Mr. Willis?"

"No," I said quickly. "You're more my type than he is. I just
thought that talking to you would be a good way of starting
the day off right."

"Why, thank you," she said. "I'll do even better—I'll wish
you good luck. Are you going to start working now?"

"You might call it that."

"What are you going to do?" she asked. "Or shouldn't I
ask that?"

"You may," I said. "Nothing."

"But—I don't understand."

"It's simple," I said. "If a guy like me comes into a strange
town and starts trying to dig up the kind of dirt your committee wants, he'll get about as far as a guy going to Las Vegas

---

* "Frammis" was a used as a surname or invented company name in comic books
of the 1940s.

with his own dice. But if he doesn't do anything, then every-body starts worrying. Sometimes they start worrying even before they see he isn't doing anything. When they get worried, they start bracing themselves. I don't push the way they're expecting me to, so they're off balance. The only problem is to keep them off balance like that long enough."

"It sounds fascinating," she said, "but how will it work in this case?"

"I'll tell you what," I said, getting around to my chief reason for calling. "After I get through putting in a hard day, why don't you meet me for dinner? Maybe I can even give you a—"

"Just a minute, Milo," she interrupted. "I've got another call coming in."

It didn't sound like a brush-off, so I waited. After a bit she came back on the wire.

"I'm sorry," she said. "Now, what were you saying?"

"You know damn well what I was saying, honey," I said.

She laughed again. "I'll be glad to have dinner with you, Milo. Where and when?"

"I'm not sure where I'll be," I said, "so let's make it about seven-thirty. Wherever you say. It's your town."

"How about the Cassandra Club?" she said. "It's on Wilson Boulevard."

"Fine. The Cassandra Club it is. At seven-thirty. I'll see you then, honey."

I hung up and decided it was time to get ready. I opened my suitcase and took out the shoulder holster and a snub-nosed .32. I buckled on the holster, slipped the gun into it, and put on my coat. It fitted the way it was supposed to.

I had another thought. I took my spare gun from the suit-case. It wasn't time to need it, but I didn't want any tourists copping it while going through my luggage. It was a gun I'd picked up at an auction years ago, an old "belly gun" with four revolving barrels. The handle was ivory, brown from age. I'd had a gunsmith fix it up for me and now it fired regular .32 shells. It looked like a museum piece, but it carried just as much punch as the new ones.

I went into the kitchen and took down a box of crackers. I emptied out most of the crackers, put the gun in the box, and put some crackers on top of it. Then I left the box sitting out on the table.

I took the bottle of brandy, a glass, and a pitcher of water into the living room. There was a small radio beside the big chair. I got a disk jockey show and sprawled out in the chair. March was working.

The disk jockey was doing an all-Ellington show and the brandy was old, so I enjoyed myself.

It was after eleven when the knock finally came on the door. I switched off the radio, transferred the glass to my left hand, and went to the door. I opened it.

He was a natty little thing. Young, maybe no more than twenty-two or three. He was wearing an expensive suit, cut a little too fancy and with too much padding in the shoulders. It made him look bigger than the five-six he probably was, until you looked close at the padding. His face was kind of pretty, if you liked the type. At first glance I thought he was a nance. But then, even before he started talking, I saw that was wrong. He was just a neat little man who was determined to prove that he was as tough as any of the big men. And he probably was, at that.

He was smoking a long, expensive cigarette and he talked around it. Not that he was wasting any words.

"Milo March?" he asked. His voice was under wraps and you could see he was always remembering to talk as much like a gentleman as he could.

I nodded.

He crowded past me into the apartment. He did it without any hint of being rough or pushing me to one side, but just the same he wasn't stopped by my halfhearted attempt to block the door. And he got in and past me without quite turning his back, but without obviously facing me. I kind of admired the skill.

I shut the door and we looked at each other. He had one of those faces that are always buttoned up. Then I saw his eyes. They were looking at me all right and not missing anything, but you could have gotten the idea that he wasn't looking anywhere. You read a lot of stories about the eyes of killers, sometimes they're steely and sometimes they're deadly, but it's all a lot of hogwash. It was when I saw this boy's eyes that I knew he was the real article. He was looking at me with the same expression he'd looked at the furniture, during the one second he'd glanced around the room and placed everything. I began to rearrange my ideas.

Just the quality of him gave me a pretty good idea of who had sent him. But he wasn't talking yet, so I made the first move.

"It's your visit," I said. "Care to tell me who you are, or should I start guessing?"

"Rudy Cioppa," he said. He didn't expect me to recognize it and he didn't care. "Johnny wants to see you."

I played it straight, just like I didn't know. "Johnny?" I asked brightly. "I don't think I know any Johnnies. Or was I too drunk to remember?"

He wasn't amused. "Johnny Doll."

I thought it over. "Never heard of him," I said, but it wasn't a very good reading.

"Don't be funny. Johnny Doll wants to see you. Now."

"How's he want me—standing up or stretched out?"

"He doesn't care. Take your pick."

"That seems fair," I said. I wasn't feeling as bright as I sounded. "I think I'll go standing up."

He was looking at the left side of my coat, at the spot just over the shoulder holster. "You loaded?" he asked.

I flipped my coat enough for him to see the leather.

"I'll take it," he said.

I could feel my stomach muscles bunching, and I was glad I'd had the brandy. I shook my head.

"I'll keep it," I said. "I'm used to it. I might get lopsided if I didn't have it."

Even then his expression didn't change. But the atmosphere in the room did. It tightened up.

"Think you can take me?" he asked.

"Maybe, maybe not," I said. "But I can try. Somewhere along the line you have to learn that I'm not just anybody's cherry to be plucked when you feel like it. I'm not pushing it, but if it has to be right here, then that's the way it is."

He didn't say anything.

"I'm not gunning for anybody," I said. I was watching his right shoulder for the first twinge. "I got all the reputation I want and I ain't collecting notches. But the gun stays. ... I knew a guy once who went out in the snow without over-shoes. He got pneumonia."

He thought it over. He couldn't find a challenge in it anywhere and it was the kind of thinking he understood. Finally he nodded. My stomach went partway back to normal.

"Okay," he said. He motioned toward the door. "Let's go. But make it easy on yourself."

And that's the way we went. Me ahead and him behind. I went as carefully as if I were walking across a sea of eggs while wearing hobnailed boots. As a matter of fact, I wanted to see Johnny Doll as much as he wanted to see me. I had known that there'd be somebody around from Johnny Doll or Jan Lomer. I wanted to see them and get straightened out on what I was looking for and how far I was looking. At the same time, it might make the man I did want just a little more nervous. But I had to be careful not to let Johnny Doll's hoods push me around too much, or everybody would get the idea it could be fun.

When we reached the street, I stopped. Carefully.

"Your car or mine?" I asked over my shoulder.

"Your car," he said.

We walked across to the Cadillac and I got in behind the steering wheel. He slipped in beside me, turning partway in the seat to face me. He put his right arm up on the window so that it looked real casual. But his fingertips were even closer to his left coat lapel. I looked at him.

"Go ahead," he said. "I'll tell you when to turn."

I started the Cadillac and we drove off. As we pulled away from the curb, I looked into the rearview mirror and saw another car following us out into the street. We were taking both his car and mine.

We headed away from the ocean, going toward Hollywood. When we were almost to the city limits, he motioned me to the curb. We braked to a stop in front of a swanky haberdashery store. I turned off the motor and looked at him.

"Out," he said. He was certainly saving with words. I wondered what he was going to do with all the words he was saving but decided I wouldn't ask.

We got out of the car and he motioned me toward the store.

"You mean Johnny Doll's in the store?" I asked.

"Yeah. He's got an office in the back."

It was a long speech for him, so I decided to see if he could keep it up.

"Ain't it kind of public?" I asked as we crossed the sidewalk. "Even if he's got a back room, customers are liable to hang around just out of curiosity."

"Not here," he said, and for the first time I thought I caught some expression in his voice. The expression was amusement.

We entered the store. It looked like any other high-priced men's store, but the clerk back of the counter didn't look like any clerk. Although he was twice the size of Rudy Cioppa, he still looked like his twin. It was partly the clothes and partly the way his face was set. He was reading a racing form and looked up as we came in. He was looking at me, but his gaze was so impersonal I felt just like an entry in the fifth at Santa Anita.

"Manny discourages customers when we ain't in the mood," Rudy said. "That's the door straight ahead."

I could see where Manny could discourage customers, so I dropped the questions and kept on going. Just as I reached the door, Rudy slipped around ahead of me. He palmed open the door and moved inside without ever losing sight of me. The boy was good.

"Here he is, Johnny," he said over his shoulder. He motioned me in. "He's got iron on him. He didn't want to shed it, so I humored him. Want me to unload him now?"

The man at the desk looked up. He was easy to recognize. Johnny Doll had had a lot of publicity, most of it naming him as one of the top fifteen or twenty racket boys in the country. He'd had his picture in *Time* and *Newsweek,* as well as in the newspapers. He'd been a star performer, without saying much, on television for the Senate Crime Commission. He was medium height, heavyset. About forty. His face was swarthy and petulant.

"It's okay, Rudy," he said. He gave me a grin. "Glad to see you, March. I've heard a lot about you."

"It seems to me I've run into your name once or twice, too," I said.

He liked it enough to broaden his grin. You could see that he was the kind of a guy who probably kept a scrapbook. Bound in white leather.

"Yeah, I've been around," he said. You could see he was proud of it. "I hear you're going to clean up Aragon City, March."

"Where'd you hear that?"

"You know how it is," he said with a careless wave of his hand. There was a diamond on one finger that looked as bright as one of the searchlights they use to announce the opening of a California hotdog stand. "I hear things here and there. I even know you arrived here a day earlier than the Civic Betterment Committee thinks you did. Why was that?"

"I like to get the lay of the land before I report," I said.

"The lay of the land, huh?" He guffawed suddenly. He continued to noisily appreciate his own joke, and I let him have a couple of chuckles just to be polite.

"Okay," he said when he'd milked the joke. "What are you going to do about Aragon City, March?"

"Not much," I admitted. "I'm hired to uncover the politician in Aragon City who's been taking a little folding money for protection, or whatever it is he's peddling. Beyond him, I'm not interested."

"But what about me?" he asked. Suddenly, he didn't look petulant or humorous. "What about Johnny Doll, huh?"

"I ain't lost anybody named Johnny Doll and I ain't looking for anybody by that name," I said. "I'm after one guy and I don't give a damn who pays him or why."

"Yeah, but maybe you can't get him without stumbling over some other things."

"I know," I said. "It's like walking a tightwire—and a pretty thin one at that. But I'm walking it. I told the Committee that's the limit of what I'd do. I've got a short nose and I'm nearsighted as hell."

He was frowning. "Even so, maybe I don't like it. You ever think of that?"

"I've thought of it," I admitted.

We looked at each other some more. Out of the corner of my eye, I could see that Rudy was looking at me too. It was a toss-up which one made me the most nervous.

"How much dough do you want?" Johnny Doll suddenly asked.

"No dough," I said. "It would only put me in a higher income bracket. I can't afford it."

He looked me over. You could see he was almost reading the price label on my suit, counting the bills in my pocket.

"An honest john, huh," he said. His voice wasn't pinning any medals on me. "Well, there are other ways. I hear you're a right guy in some ways, so I'll put it to you straight. I want you to lay off Aragon City. I'd even like it if you got out of town. Quick."

I didn't like the way this was going, but there wasn't much I could do about it.

"If you've heard so much about me," I said, "then you should have heard that I don't quit on a job. I'm sorry, Johnny, but that's the way it is."

"Okay. Like I said, there are other ways." He didn't take his eyes off me. "Want to show him one of the ways, Rudy?"

The little guy didn't answer, but he started moving toward me. Slowly. His right hand went into his coat pocket, and when he took it out, the light reflected from the metal. Knuckle dusters.

This was going to be a tough one to handle all around.

One kind of wrong move and the whole town could explode around my ears. Another kind of wrong move and March would go out like a lamb—in the slaughterhouse. I didn't have any clear idea how to handle it, but I started backing off. Rudy kept coming, no change in his expression. His eyes gave me the creeps.

I felt the wall touch my shoulders and that was that. I waited.

Rudy stopped in front of me and studied my face like it was a wall and he was trying to think of the best place to drive the nail. Then he swung.

I waited until the last possible moment, then slipped to one side. His fist slid past my face and hit the wall. There was the crunching sound of steel and plaster, but part of it was the sound of flesh.

Even then he never changed expression. I was watching his face to see, and it was like watching a scoreboard before the game starts. He didn't even blink. He just backed away and looked at me. He stripped the steel from his hand and tossed it to the floor. There was blood running down his fingers.

"Okay," he said flatly. "So you're fast on your feet." He moved the fingers of his right hand experimentally. They worked all right. His hand moved slowly up toward his left shoulder.

I got tense again. He was going for his gun and Johnny Doll wasn't saying anything. I figured he didn't intend to shoot me there—it'd be bad for the shirt business. A pistol whipping was probably on his mind, but I didn't intend to take that either. I sneaked a look at Johnny Doll. One hand was out of sight below the desk. It looked like it was going to be table stakes with the odds two to one. A sucker's game—but, like the old story, it was the only game in town.

I was saved by the bell. The phone rang.

"Hold it, Rudy," Johnny Doll said. His voice was thick and I knew I'd guessed it right. Rudy Cioppa stayed just the way he was. Johnny picked up the phone and said hello.

Whoever it was did most of the talking. Johnny kept saying "Yeah," mostly as if he didn't like what he was hearing. After about three minutes of this, he banged the receiver back on the hook.

"Now?" Rudy asked. The little man hadn't moved.

"No," Johnny Doll said. He sounded unhappy, so I began to relax. He was looking at me again, but his face was once more petulant and I guessed that was good for me. I'd guessed right.

"March," he said, "you ever hear of Jan Lomer?"

"I've heard of him," I said cautiously.

"He wants to see you."

So that was it. Jan Lomer was the other half of the Syndicate team in Aragon City. It was my hunch that he was the important half. The phone call must have been from him and he must have said no rough stuff. So I had another chance to get them to lay off while I did my work.

"Okay," I said. "Where does he live?"

"Out in Crestwood Canyon. Rudy will take you out."

"If you don't mind," I said, "give me the address and I'll find it myself."

"What's the matter with Rudy showing you?"

"He makes me nervous," I said truthfully.

That tickled them. Johnny Doll laughed. Rudy's face had something that might have passed for a grin on a dark night.

"It's Four Twenty Marisol Drive," Johnny said. He winked at Rudy, but I pretended not to see it. "I guess you're a big boy, so go by yourself. Just one thing, March—remember what I said. I don't like you gunning around in my territory."

"I'll remember," I said seriously. It made him feel better, which was what I wanted. There was one important lesson I learned early. With guys like Johnny Doll and Rudy Cioppa, you can get along with them if you can keep them from feeling they have to do something about you to save face.

I turned to go. Rudy was standing beside the door, rubbing the dried blood from his knuckles.

"I'll remember too," he said to me. "I owe you one."

"Take your time about paying it," I said lightly. "I know you're good for it. I'll see you boys around."

"*We'll* be around all right," Johnny Doll said. His meaning was clear enough, so I didn't answer.

It was the little guy I worried about anyway. Ever since I'd first seen him, I'd had a hunch that sooner or later he and I would tangle. If nothing else, sooner or later he'd start worrying about the fact that I hadn't let him take my gun. Then he'd have to find out if he *could* take it.

I walked through the store and out to the Cadillac. I knew the general direction of Crestwood Canyon, so I headed for it. In the meantime I fished a directory from the compartment and by taking quick glances I located the section and the street. It was after I put the directory away that I noticed the car following me. It was the same one that had followed me down. The boys were checking up to see if I went to visit Jan Lomer. That was okay too.

The address turned out to be a huge Colonial-style house on what could only be called an estate. The lawn was as big as a couple of city blocks and was filled with flower beds. There were plenty of trees too. An old-fashioned grilled iron fence embraced the whole place. Looking at it, I grinned. The guy who made up that slogan "Crime doesn't pay" should have seen that place.

I drove through the open gate and up to the house. It had a circular driveway. Everything looked peaceful and legal. But I noticed that off to one side there was a small concrete building, made to look like an old-time well house. I was willing to bet there was a guy in there loaded with more than the old oaken bucket.

I left the car in the driveway and went up to the front door. It was an old-fashioned door too, but I noticed that something new had been added. There was a peephole. It was made to look decorative, but that's what it was.

I manipulated the brass knocker and waited. I pretended to ignore the movement at the peephole. Then there was another wait and the door opened. The man who stood there was big. He was fat too, but he would have still been big if you'd taken all the fat from him. He was wearing an expensive-looking smoking jacket, and the face above it was intelligent. It might have been the face of an old man who'd spent a life poring over books, but there was nothing nearsighted about the eyes. He was maybe sixty or sixty-five.

Jan Lomer was different from Johnny Doll. He'd had his

share of publicity, but there was never as much of it. When-ever his picture appeared in a newspaper or magazine, it always just happened that he was raising his arm, removing his hat, or doing something that hid his face. He'd never been arrested, so there were no cop-posed pictures of him.

Even though I'd never seen him, I knew that this was Jan Lomer standing in the doorway. This was another difference between him and Johnny. He was coming to the door himself instead of sending a hood.

"Mr. March?" he asked. His voice was deep and sounded as if he was straining to force it through his throat.

"Yeah," I said. "You're Jan Lomer?"

"I am. It was kind of you, Mr. March, to come here to see an old man. Very kind of you."

"Not at all," I said. "At the moment you called to invite me, I was being entertained by Rudy Cioppa. So your invitation wasn't exactly unwelcome."

He laughed. It was a wheezing gush of sound. Like his speech, it sounded as if he had to strain to get it out.

"Ah, yes," he said, "Rudy is sometimes a bit abrupt as a host. Come in, Mr. March, come in."

I stepped past him into the hallway. I waited until he closed the door and then followed him down the hall and into a study. It was big enough to make a whole house for some people. Three of the walls were lined with books from the ceiling to the floor. And they looked well read. Some people have books and you can tell at a glance that they want you to think they're intellectual, though all they ever read are comics.

Jan Lomer stepped around and sat down at the desk. He motioned me to a huge leather chair in front of the desk. I sat down and got out a cigarette.

"I was about to have lunch, Mr. March," he said. "Will you join me?"

I realized I was getting hungry. I nodded.

"Eggs Benedict?" he asked. I nodded again. "Something to drink, Mr. March?"

"Brandy," I said. "With the coffee."

He nodded. There was an intercom on his desk. He spoke into it, then leaned back in his chair. He picked up a silver cup from his desk and fondled it.

"Mr. March," he said, "do you know what this is?"

I had noticed it before. Now I looked at it more closely. It was a tall silver cup, almost every inch of it covered with fine engraving. I couldn't make out all the detail, but I could see it was beautiful work.

"It looks like a Cellini," I said, "but that's impossible, so it must be an imitation. A good one."

"Why impossible, Mr. March?"

"Because there's no such cup by Cellini in existence." I searched my memory. "The known works of Cellini are the famous salt cellar, a medallion of Clement VII, a medal of Francis I, a medal of Cardinal Pietro Bembo—"

"No need to run through the list," he interrupted. "Here, Mr. March. Look at it."

He handed me the silver cup. I turned it over in my hands. The more I looked, the more I was amazed. It must have shown in my face. He chuckled.

"You see, Mr. March," he said, "it is not an imitation. That is the silver cup Cellini made for the Cardinal of Ferrara."

"I've heard of it," I said, "but there's never been a single report of its being in existence. Nothing's known of it since it was first made."

"Exactly, sir." He reached out and I put the silver cup in his hand. "Not only do I own it, sir, but I am the only man living who knows the history of this cup. It is a unique history, Mr. March."

"It must be, if there's never been anything printed on it."

"This cup, sir," he said, "has changed hands thirty-one times since it was created. I am the thirty-second person to own it. Not one of the exchanges has been … shall we say, legal. And in twenty-four cases the owner was murdered in order to facilitate the transfer of ownership. I intend, Mr. March, to break this chain of events."

"You mean to sell it?"

"Unthinkable, sir! But I expect to keep it as long as I live. And I intend, sir, to die a natural death. At that time, the cup will go to an art museum. … But you amaze me, Mr. March."

"Yeah?" I asked.

"As you might imagine," he said, "I've met a number of representatives of the law in my time. But you, Mr. March, are the first cop—you'll pardon the expression—I've ever met who could recognize the work of Cellini. Most of them never get beyond the illustrations in *Grushenka*."*

"I've seen that, too," I said. I looked at him. "I've met a lot

---

* *Grushenka: Three Times a Woman* (1933) is a work of bawdy erotic fiction set in Tsarist Russia.

of representatives of the underworld in my time. But you, Mr. Lomer, are the first crook—*you'll* pardon the expression—I've ever met who *owned* a work of Cellini."

He laughed until the desk shook.

The door opened and a man came in. He was dressed like a servant, but he didn't look the part. He was wheeling a serving table. There were two trays on it with covered plates. There were a big silver coffee pot and cups and saucers, and a bottle of brandy with two inhalers. He served the food to us and left.

"Look, Mr. Lomer—" I began.

"Mr. March," he interrupted, "I prefer not to talk business during lunch. I believe you will find the Eggs Benedict are superb. I have an excellent chef, and his food deserves your full attention."

The Eggs Benedict *were* good. I couldn't remember any that were better.

"How do you keep him?" I asked. "The chef. I've always heard the good ones are nervous. I'd think that having guys like Rudy Cioppa around would upset him."

"In this case, sir, you might call it a steadying influence," he said. "My chef developed at one time the unfortunate habit of using a cleaver on employers who were so rash as to not appreciate his sauces."

"Then be sure to give him my compliments," I said, turning back to the eggs. He laughed again.

We'd finished the eggs and I was working on the brandy and coffee before he spoke again.

"Mr. March," he said, "I like you. I see no reason why we shouldn't get along splendidly."

I nodded and kept on appreciating the brandy.

"You, Mr. March," he continued, "have been employed by the Aragon City Civic Betterment Committee. The purpose of the employment is to find the man with whom Johnny Doll and I do business. Correct, sir?"

"Yeah," I said, "and that's all. There's nothing in my contract that says I have to hang Johnny Doll and Jan Lomer up by the heels."

"Excellent. At the same time, sir, you'll appreciate the fact that your investigation might prove ... shall we say, embarrassing to us."

"If you're afraid I'll get in your hair," I said, "why don't we make a deal? You hand me the guy on a platter, my work will be over, and I'll leave."

"I'm afraid not, sir," he said. "Not that I have any sentimental attachment to the man. Honor among thieves, sir, is a lot of balderdash. But it might make it difficult to do business with others. If you are successful in your mission, I foresee no difficulty in making arrangements with someone in the new administration. I'm being frank with you, sir."

"What happens with the new administration is none of my business," I said.

"Mr. March," he said, "I have taken the trouble of looking into your personal history. You have the reputation of always keeping your word. Now, sir, will you give me your word that our enterprises will be left alone?"

I finished my brandy and observed two minutes of silence out of respect.

"Maybe," I said finally. "First, Johnny Doll has some idea of pushing me around. And Rudy Cioppa wants to do the push-ing. I don't like it. When I'm pushed, I'm liable to push back."

"Most understandable, sir. I think I can promise you that you will not be harmed once you've given me your word."

"Okay," I said. "Next question: what are your enterprises? I don't want to be accused of breaking my word if I happen to push a crooked cop in the face or if I fall into bed with a girl who's undercutting the local Syndicate price."

The laugher rumbled deep in his throat. "I like you, Mr. March," he said again. "I'm beginning to understand why you're fond of Cellini. ... I'll be frank, sir—just between the two of us here. Our enterprises, sir, consist of every bit of gambling in Aragon City and quite a bit of it in other spots. This includes punchboards, pinball machines, slot machines when we can get away with them, the wheel houses, floating crap games, horse parlors and bookies, the numbers, and one gambling ship out beyond the three-mile limit."

"That must provide a tidy little income," I said.

"We find it satisfactory," he said. "Then you might say we have a monopoly on the more exotic stimulants. Marijuana, opium, heroin, morphine, cocaine." He sounded like a hard-ware wholesaler listing the items he carried.

"What about the notch houses?"

"We participate in the sex traffic."

"I thought you had a finger in that," I said.

He laughed until the tears came to his eyes. "But no more than that, sir," he said. "I'm an old man." He laughed some more.

It wasn't that good a joke, but who was I to spoil his fun.

"We own," he said when he got through yukking it up, "about fifty percent of the houses and the call numbers. In the rest, we book the talent. We own or control the nude studios, the picture business, and the stag movies. We also book most of the stag parties."

I really didn't care about all this, but I was fascinated by the way he reeled it off. "What about murder?" I wanted to know.

He shook his head. "No murder, sir," he said, "unless it's absolutely necessary. When it is, that's out of my department." I knew without asking that was Johnny Doll's end. "Mr. March, we try to operate without violence. That was one of the major errors of those in this profession years ago. We pay our income tax, we discourage violence of any sort, and to a large extent we keep the city clear of heist mobs. You might say that we're not without benefit to the community."

"I might," I said, without bothering to add that I wouldn't. "One more thing, Mr. Lomer. When I get the man you're paying for protection—and I will get him—there's liable to be a payoff man in the net. Maybe I can't do anything about that."

"It had already occurred to me, sir." He stared at me for a minute. "Mr. March, when you're sure you have your man, come to me. Then we will provide a sacrificial lamb to lie down with your lion."

"Fair enough," I said. Actually, the only thing I wanted to be sure about was that they laid off me. Some guys in this business get delusions of grandeur, but I know better than to think that one guy can buck a whole Syndicate that stretches from New York to Los Angeles, with maybe one arm in Italy. "I give you my word, Mr. Lomer."

"Excellent," he said. "Mr. March, I don't mind telling you that we will be just as happy to see things change in Aragon City. You understand we buy our protection from one man, but those with whom he in turn arranges the protection have been getting a little out of hand. I tell you, sir, there is nothing worse than a crooked cop."

"You ought to know," I said. "You make them that way."

"Hazards of the profession, sir," he said. "Will you join me in another brandy?"

"I'd like to," I said, "but I'd better set a few more wheels in motion." I stood up. "I'm curious about something."

"Go ahead, sir," he said.

"I've been around," I said, "and I've met a lot of racket boys. All of them have been hoods to some degree or other. Some of them were nice guys, some weren't, but they were still hoods. If they read anything, it was comics. If they thought about anything, it was either dames or how to muscle in on a new racket. In many ways, you're different. What are you doing in a mug's racket?"

He leaned back in his chair and beamed at me. It was obvious that he'd given it a lot of thought and the answer was something he enjoyed giving.

"Mr. March," he said, "we live in a corrupt society. And I, sir, am a part of that society. To pretend otherwise would mean being hypocritical. Ethically, sir, there is no difference between the observer and the participant. By taking a more active part in the corruption of our society, I am able to surround myself with things which give me pleasure. I sell corruption, sir, in a society which is eager to buy it—with the profit obtained, I buy objects of beauty. This cup by Cellini, a private art collection which is one of the finest in the country, my books—I have some excellent first editions and original manuscripts. To paraphrase the Tentmaker, sir, I often wonder what a man could sell one half so wonderful as the things he can buy." *

"Very pretty," I said. I decided to push him a little farther. "But did you ever reckon up the cost in tokens other than money? Do you ever look at the Cellini cup, say, and think how much it costs in drug addicts, in men and women who lose their security over the gambling tables, in girls lying on their backs with their eyes shut, their fists clenched, their teeth on edge?"

He'd thought about it, all right. He didn't like thinking about it either. He picked up the silver cup and rubbed it automatically, as if trying to remove stains.

"Mr. March," he said heavily, "you are a disappointment to me. I've thought of it, sir. I know of a man in Aragon City who also owns an original Cellini. He is a banker, sir, a respected member of our society. One of his important holdings is a block of shares in a distilling corporation. There are, sir, more alcoholics in this country than drug addicts. Business has been good for him the last year because of the increase in real estate values. He has been able to foreclose the mortgages on a number of veterans' homes and sell them at higher prices. I might add, sir, that he also owns the mortgages on five of our whorehouses. Do you see my point, Mr. March?"

---

* This paraphrase is the reverse of the couplet "I often wonder what the Vintners buy/One half so precious as the stuff they sell" from the *Rubaiyat* of Omar Khayyam (the Tentmaker). The poet cannot imagine that people who sell wine could buy with their profits anything more valuable than the joy of drink itself.

"I see it, all right," I said. "But it's not much of a point. The banker being wrong doesn't make you right. ... I'll be seeing you around, Mr. Lomer."

"Just a minute, sir. I have not finished."

"Okay. What else?"

"I mentioned, Mr. March, that I am a part of a corrupt society. Do not make the error of thinking that I am all of it. You, sir, came to me as an individual who has been hired to end the corruption in Aragon City. You consider me the chief influence in this corruption, yet you have just given me your word that you will not touch the enterprises which I represent. You, sir, would toss a pebble at a Pygmy and pretend that you are David slaying Goliath. You disappoint me, Mr. March."

"You know, you've got something there," I said. He did, too. I stared at him thoughtfully. "Wouldn't it be funny if you talked me into cracking down on you, too?"

"Not at all, sir," he said. Some of his gentleness had dropped from him. "It would be unfortunate. I like you, Mr. March, and I would like to think that a man sensitive enough to appreciate Cellini is also aware that it's better to be a corrupt member of society—than a dead one."

"I'll think it over," I said. There wasn't much else to say. He'd gotten the best of the argument. Maybe I should have stuck to dealing with Rudy. He didn't cover his boobytraps with a lot of words.

I said good-bye and went out to the Cadillac.

THREE

I drove toward the ocean at a leisurely pace. I had started the conversation with Jan Lomer with the idea of jolting him, but I'd gotten the charge instead. He'd been completely right. Finding the politician who was giving the rackets protection wouldn't mean a thing. They'd find somebody in the new administration who'd provide the same service for the same price. Organized crime represented so much money that they could always buy someone, no matter what his price was.

I didn't have the answer to the problem. I hadn't done much thinking about it, but I realized this was one of the reasons I hadn't wanted the job. Normally, I go along doing my regular job, finding lost, strayed, and stolen jewelry, sometimes dickering with the people who took it, sometimes finding ways of bringing pressure on them. A few times I'd taken jobs like this one, but I'd never liked them.

I was pretty annoyed with myself for ever starting that talk about ethics. When I looked at my own, I had only two choices. I could get the man who was providing protection for the Syndicate and shut my eyes to the rest of the mess, or I could try to clean up the whole town and find myself leading a slow-marching parade to the nearest cemetery.

To hell with it. I pulled the Cadillac in to the curb and went into a drugstore. I leafed through the phone book until I found the address of the old lady, Elizabeth Saxon. I got back in the Cadillac and headed for it.

Some people might have gotten the idea that I wasn't working very hard. People like that read too many books. They think investigators investigate. They've got mental pictures of some guy, who always looks like Howard Duff, wearing a trench coat, going around and peering through keyholes and digging up a lot of bright, shining clues. But it never works out like that. I wouldn't know a clue if I stepped on one.

Officially I had been in Aragon City about eighteen hours; unofficially, twenty-four hours longer. I had a pretty fair picture of the city. Like a lot of other towns, it was pretty well dirtied up. It wasn't crime-ridden in the sense of robbery and organized murder; it was up to here in gambling, dope, and prostitutes. A small part of the cops were crooked, but they were the only cops who could do anything about it. The criminals were sort of half respectable—even when they were attacked in the newspapers, the results usually glamorized them. A lot of kids thought more about aping them than the quieter members of society. Everyone knew about it, but no one felt there was anything he could do about it. Certain kinds of crime were already on the way to being accepted as part of society.

I knew the town. I'd made a sort of peace with the Syndicate so there wouldn't be a lot of hoods breathing down the back of my neck every time I took a step. The other half of the team—the crooked cops and the crooked politicians—were worried. I had figured they were the ones who'd sent the call girl the night before. It was the kind of frame that only a cop would think up. The Syndicate boys would never send a girl to do a hood's work. And I had already smoked out two of this half—the two cops who had visited me. They were small fry, but as soon as they got more worried there'd be someone bigger. They'd try more frames, and all I had to do was watch my step until they hung themselves in it.

It was a little like making a target of yourself until somebody's gun jammed between shots and he'd look down the barrel.

I parked in front of the old lady's address. It was a big house and you could see that maybe thirty years before it had been the showplace of the West Coast. Now it was old but still in good condition. But the neighborhood had changed. All around the mansion were rooming houses; they were crowding in on the old girl, but she was standing her ground.

The door was opened by a butler who must have been all of eighty. He was hard of hearing too, but on the third try he got my name. He showed me into a room that was like taking a time machine back to the last century. Even the pictures on the walls were of old guys sporting beavers and high choker collars. He left me there with someone else's memories.

When she came into the room, she was dressed so that she seemed a part of it. The only things out of place there were me and the twinkle in her eye.

"Well, young man," she said, "I was hoping you'd come to see me. It isn't often that young men call on an old lady."

"Don't give me that old lady stuff," I said. "You've got more life than anyone else on that committee of yours."

She gave me a genteel smile, but her eyes said she liked it more than that.

"Can I have Jarvis bring you a drink?" she asked. "Father always served the men bourbon, and we still have some left."

"I'm a brandy man myself," I said. "But don't let me keep you from having one."

"Ladies of my generation never drank," she said. She gave me that smile. "Although I'll never know why. I've come to enjoy bourbon since I got up enough nerve to try it. ... What can I do for you, Mr. March?"

"I don't know," I said honestly. "I'm just floating around, picking up what I can." I got out a cigarette and looked at her. She nodded and I lit it. "How did this Civic Betterment Committee get started?"

"I started it," she said promptly. "I gave the rest of them the choice of coming along or having me clean up the town by myself."

"I'll bet you did at that," I said. I looked her over. I decided I'd needle her a little. "You want the town all cleaned up," I said. "No drinking, no little card games, no boy and girl stuff. Maybe everybody going to church every Sunday."

"Nonsense," she said sharply. "I merely object to my city being run by a pack of hoodlums, and I don't like the idea of city officials being bought like so much beef. The only thing I'd do away with, Mr. March, is the sale of drugs. But if people want to gamble, let them do so in their own homes and for stakes they can afford. If the men want women, let them go to the amateurs. God knows there's plenty of them in Aragon City." She looked at me brightly. "I have nothing against whores," she said. "I know plenty of respectable women who married their husbands for their money."

I grinned. "You say what you think, don't you?"

"It's a privilege of being old and rich," she said. "Mr. March, I never had any fun in my life. I never even knew how people had fun until I was too old for such things. Now I own half of this town. So I'm going to be honest, if it kills everyone else."

"And it probably will," I said. "Why did the Committee want to hire me?"

"I made them," she said.

"How did you know about me?"

"One of my secret vices," she said, "is reading true detective magazines. I read a story in one once about another city hiring you to do the same kind of job. I liked the description of you, so we hired you."

I nodded. That cleared up the reason why Linn Willis wouldn't take no for an answer, yet never showed any great enthusiasm for me. I'd wondered about that.

"What can you tell me about the rest of the Committee?" I asked.

"I've known most of them since they were children," she said. "Linn Willis prides himself on being a self-made man. He's an honest man who is a little bit afraid to tamper with things, because in some way it might hurt him. But he likes his money and power enough to buckle down when it's a pinch. George Stern would like to go into politics, so he's trying not to offend anyone, but he'd like some publicity. Donald Reid is a pious old idiot. He'll do what he's told and that's all. Sherman Marshall is an old windbag. Dr. Jilton is on the Committee because he likes to keep in with the best people."

"And Miss Russell?"

The old lady snorted. "She's decoration," she said. "Linn Willis brought her to the Committee. Good for publicity, he said. But you should know more about her than I do, young man. I saw the way the two of you looked at each other."

I almost blushed. That hadn't happened in twenty years. I changed the subject.

"Who do you think is providing the protection in Aragon City?" I asked.

"I don't know," she said. "It might be Leo Gibbs. He's chief of police. When he was a boy, he worked for my father. Father always suspected him of stealing."

"That doesn't mean anything," I said. "Lots of kids steal because they haven't anything else to do." I thought about it for a minute. "You know," I said, "there are a lot of politicians who have a sixth sense when it comes to knowing which way the wind is blowing. And by now it's no secret what your committee wants to do. Whoever has been giving protection to Johnny Doll and Jan Lomer is getting rich from it. He won't want to give it up. So he'd take steps to be on the winning team, no matter who wins. Now, he may or may not be a politician. But if he is one, it's interesting that the one member of the present political administration who is a member of your committee is the Commissioner of Parks, Sherman Marshall."

"But he's such an old fool," she said.

"You don't have to be a genius to take money."

"But how could he?" she asked. "He's only the Commissioner of Parks. How could he give protection?"

"The guy in charge of the protection could be anybody," I

said. "He might be the mayor or a street cleaner or somebody who shows no interest in politics. He has to split his take with others. Maybe the mayor, certainly the chief of police, and some of the police force. I met two of the cops last night. Harry Fleming and one named Grant."

"Gene Grant," she said. "I know both of them. They were never any good."

"Good or not," I said, "they're in on the take. But they're small fry. And the guy on top can be anybody."

She looked at me shrewdly. "Is that why you said you wouldn't report to the Committee until it was over?"

I nodded. "I'd make real fancy odds that the top man is either on the Committee or has someone on it. So until I know better, I'm trusting no one on the Committee—not even you."

That flattered her. "You know," she said, and for a minute she looked twenty years younger, "there are times when I wished I had the nerve to do something like that."

"Liz Saxon, the Queen of the Underworld," I said without cracking a smile.

She beamed. "Young man, you're corrupting me," she said. Then she stopped playing. "I never thought that someone on the Committee might be there for the reasons you mention. What about that Vega Russell?"

"Don't look now, but your jealousy is showing. You're just making noises like a cat."

"Not jealousy—envy," she said, and meant it. "Anyway, now I'll keep an eye on everyone on the Committee."

"You do that," I said. I didn't think it would really do any good, but it would keep the old lady happy.

We talked some more and then I left. I drove straight down-town and found the District Attorney's office. His name was Martin Yale. I showed the receptionist the piece of paper that said I worked for him and that got me right in.

He was maybe three or four years older than me. About forty. He had one of those rugged faces that never loses its grimness no matter how much he laughs. The rest of him was built the same way. I liked his looks and decided maybe he hadn't just made a gesture. But I wanted to find out.

"I'm Milo March," I said.

"Yes," he said. It was a simple statement of fact. He was willing to grant that I was Milo March, but he wasn't granting any more than that.

"This piece of paper," I said, waving it in front of him, "says that I'm an investigator for you. How much does that mean?"

"As much as you want it to mean," he said quietly. "It doesn't give you any free rides anywhere; it won't even get you into the movies unless you push in seventy-five cents along with it."

"I'm not looking for any rides, free or otherwise," I said. "Why did you write me a blank check like this?"

He leaned back in his chair and stared me straight in the eye. "I approve of the stated intentions of the Civic Better-ment Committee," he said. "They asked me to give you some legal status. I did a little checking, especially with the chief of police in Denver. He rated you pretty high, so you got the paper. It may be a blank check, but payment can be stopped quick."

I grinned to myself, remembering the phone call I'd had the

night before. It seemed everybody was calling Denver about me. But it was nice to know that I had recommendations from both the chief of police and the leading madam. That sort of covered all possibilities.

"How far will you back me up?" I asked him.

"If you're on the right track, all the way," he said. "If you go on the wrong one, I'll walk all over you just like I never heard of you."

"It's apt to get a little messy," I said.

He nodded as if I'd said we might have sunshine before the day was over.

"Also," I said, "I'll be limited in the proof I can get on some of them. If things stack up right, are you willing to grab safe deposit boxes, go into bank accounts, things like that?"

"Yes," he said. He bit the word off like he was already prying open locks.

"I met a couple of city cops last night," I said. "Small fry, but they were full of ambition. As the days go by, that feeling's going to creep up. Before it's over, some pretty big people are apt to have their shoulders to the wheel. How do you take pushing?"

"Mr. March," he said, "I was elected by the people and they are the only ones who can fire me." The way he said it didn't sound like a sermon. "Being a District Attorney is a dog's job, but that doesn't mean I wear a collar. There have been, however, a lot of ways my hands have been tied in cleaning up Aragon City. If you're on the level, March—and I've been made to feel you are—you'll get complete backing as long as I'm District Attorney. Does that answer your question?"

"It does," I said. I stood up. "Keep the bromide handy."

He gave me a friendly grin. "What are your plans, March?" he asked. "Or would you rather not say?"

"Can't," I said. "I don't have any plans. When you're looking for a needle in a haystack, you can't draw a picture showing which way the needle's pointing. All you can do is keep on sitting down all over the place until finally you get the point."

He laughed, which made it a good exit line, so I left.

It was three o'clock. My date with the redhead was for seven-thirty, so I decided to go back to my apartment. I could take a shower, deposit a couple of brandies, and just sit around. Something might even happen. By this time everyone knew where I lived.

I drove out to Miramar Terrace. I parked in front of the house and went upstairs. When I was putting my key in the lock, I heard the phone ringing. I opened the door and went in fast.

I automatically looked around the room as I picked up the phone. Then I had a little trouble answering, but I finally made it.

"Yeah?" I said.

"Hello, darling." It was the Canadian Club voice. "This is Polly East."

"I know," I said.

"I checked up on that business of last night," she said. "We won't mention any names, darling, but I talked to the man who asked me to send Mickie out to see you. I've told him that I won't play any more games like that. I wanted you to know, darling. Polly East runs a clean house."

"That's nice," I said flatly. I kept looking at the studio bed.

"I explained it to Mickie," she said. "She said she might come out to see you today. Has she been there yet?"

"Yes," I said.

"Good," Polly East said. "Tell her I won't take any calls for her tonight. That will give the two of you a chance to get acquainted. Mickie's a nice girl."

"Was," I said.

"What?"

"Was a nice girl," I explained carefully. "She's dead."

There was a long pause.

She said a short hard word. I waited out another pause.

"I'm sorry," she said finally. "Mickie was a swell girl—oh, hell, I guess I'd better stop talking."

She hung up.

I put the receiver back, still looking at the bed. She was lying there on the bed. Just like the night before, her clothes were over a chair. But there were a couple of differences. The night before her clothes were draped neatly over the chair. Now they were just bunched on it. And just below one of Mickie Gill's beautiful breasts there was a small blue-black hole. There wasn't much blood around it. I wondered why.

I walked over and picked up a handful of her clothes. There was plenty of blood on them. And there was a hole in the white blouse. Somebody had killed her and then taken her clothes off. I wondered about that, too. Murder was murder whether the corpse was naked or not. And a frame was a frame no matter how you dressed it. I decided that the undressing was just an extra piece of nastiness.

I walked over to the bed and looked at her. Maybe she was only a call-house girl and I didn't really know anything about her except that she was pretty, but I didn't like this. Not only because it was a frame. She'd gone through enough without the final obscenity of someone shoving a bullet through her.

I leaned over and looked closer at the bullet hole. I prodded at the flesh with a forefinger. She'd been dead for a while, but maybe not long enough to pull off the frame. I knew I didn't have much time. There was no point in trying to beat it. But maybe it was time to call on Martin Yale for some of that backing. I moved over to the phone. I figured I had just about enough time to call the D.A.

I was wrong.

I'd locked the door, but this time they had a key. They came in fast without any nonsense about knocking. It was the same two as the night before. They didn't look surprised at the sight of the body on the bed. I didn't expect them to.

"Hold it," the skinny one said. He had a gun in his hand. I let my hand drift away from the phone.

"Well, well, Harry," he said. "Looks like we stumbled onto something."

"Yeah," the paunchy one said. He walked across the room and looked down at the girl. When he looked up at me, I could see he was enjoying himself.

"Pretty nice, huh?" he said, grinning.

I wanted to hit him, but I knew they'd like that. So I just stood there, not even breathing any more than I had to.

"I'll bet she was hot stuff," he said. "Why did you cool her?"

"It wasn't that," I said tightly. "She looked out the window and saw you. She thought it was better to commit suicide than to ever have to see such a face again."

"I'm going to like working over you," he said. "You're one of those enameled guys. I like to watch it crack off."

"I'll bet you do," I said. "Even better than girls, huh?" That got him a little. Not much, but he tightened a little around the eyes.

"Better look him over, Harry," the other one said. He was still holding the gun on me. "He's probably got the gun still on him."

The paunchy one moved around behind me. He was careful, all right. He patted me all around, moving up to my shoulder. He reached around my left arm and took the gun from my holster. As he brought it out, he lifted it so the barrel raked my jaw. Not hard, just enough to rock me a little.

"So sorry," he said. "That was careless of me. We don't go in for rough stuff."

"Sure," I said. "Undressing a dead girl is more in your line."

He could afford to let it ride and he knew it. He moved around to the side and made a show of sniffing at the barrel of my gun.

"I guess he cleaned it right away," he said to the other cop.

"It's clean, all right," I said. "Also, you'll have a hell of a time making the bullet fit that barrel." But I was just talking. I knew all the tricks. If the murder gun was a .32 and they had it—and I was willing to bet it was and they did—then they could easily switch barrels on the two guns.

"Sure," the skinny one said. I remembered his name was Gene Grant. "All right, let's go, March."

"Where?" I asked innocently.

"We don't like killers in this town. We've got a little reception planned for you."

"What do you do with killers in Aragon City?" I asked. "Pin badges on them?"

"Get going," he said. He motioned toward the door with his gun.

"What about her?" I asked.

They both looked at her, but the one named Harry Fleming took a long look. You could tell he wasn't looking at the bullet hole.

"They'll pick her up in a basket," he said. He shook his head. "The worms are sure getting a break this time." They herded me out of the apartment.

FOUR

The precinct house looked like dozens of others. It was an old brick building, red-brown in color. There were green lights on each side of the door. Inside, it was dark after the bright sunlight outdoors. A bored-looking desk sergeant looked up as we came in.

"We've got a guest, Joe," Grant said to the desk sergeant. "Book him on an open charge."

"No, you don't," I said quickly. "You've got to charge me."

"What do you know?" Harry Fleming said. "He knows the law and everything."

"We can hold you for questioning for twenty-four hours," Grant said. "That's an open charge. And that's what we're doing."

"I want to make a phone call," I said. "That's my right."

"Sure, sure," Grant said. He exchanged grins with the desk sergeant. "You'll get your rights. Just relax while you're being booked."

The desk sergeant picked up a pen and looked at me. "Name?" he asked.

"Milo March."

He wrote it down. "Address?"

"Sixty-two Miramar Terrace."

"That's a temporary address," Grant said quickly. "He's a transient."

"Age?"

"Thirty-four."

"White," he said, writing it down. He looked at me. "Male, I guess, huh?"

Fleming snickered. "If he ain't, something in his apartment was certainly being wasted."

They all considered themselves pretty funny fellows.

"Okay," the desk sergeant said. "Empty your pockets."

I piled the stuff up on his desk. Cigarettes. Ronson lighter. Five hundred dollars in bills. A couple of bucks in change. Keys. Driving license. Gun license. Identification as a D.A.'s investigator. My Denver identification. A handkerchief. Nail file. Pencil and pen. Small notebook. Extra shells for my gun.

Grant tossed my gun on the desk beside the stuff.

"Here's his gun," he said. "Put it with the rest of the stuff. We'll send it over to ballistics later."

Harry Fleming was pawing through my stuff. He waved a slip of paper.

"What do you know," he said in mock wonderment. "He's an investigator for the D.A. Practically a cop himself."

Grant clucked. "Nothing worse than an officer of the law going wrong," he said, shaking his head.

"You boys ought to know," I said.

"Shut up," Harry Fleming said. He rubbed the knuckles of his right hand thoughtfully.

The desk sergeant listed all the stuff. After exchanging glances with the others, he finally pushed my cigarettes and the lighter back to me. Then he gave me a receipt.

"The captain in?" Grant asked the desk sergeant.

"Yeah."

"Okay, March," Grant said. "Let's go."

We went down the hall and stopped in front of a door. Grant opened the door and we went in. A big, beefy guy with a red face was sitting at a desk. He wore a uniform. He was a captain. He was on the phone as we came in.

"I know, Chief," he was saying, "but don't let it worry you. I don't like slip-ups either." There was a pause. His voice was harder when he spoke again. "I said we'll do it my way and that's how it'll be done. Just go home, put your feet in some hot water, and stop worrying. I know what I'm doing."

He hung up and looked at us.

It looked like I'd taken a big step up the ladder.

"Captain," Grant said, aping politeness, "this is Milo March. This is Captain Sam Logan, Mr. March."

"Milo March," the Captain said slowly. He was acting too. Just a bunch of kids, all of them. Tickled to death with their own cleverness. "That name sounds familiar ..."

"Maybe it's because he works for the D.A.," Grant said. "An investigator. You know, that makes him practically a real detective."

"It's a great act," I said wearily, "but the house isn't big enough to make it profitable to keep up. There's just one thing I want and then you can go back to knocking yourselves out with your stale jokes. I want to make a phone call."

"Yeah, he wants his rights," Harry Fleming said.

"You mean this man's under arrest?" the Captain asked. His astonishment wouldn't have fooled the village idiot. "Well, then, Mr. March, of course you'll get your rights. Every one of them."

"You mean I can make a call? Now?"

"Well," the Captain said, "the law says we have to either let you make a phone call or that we have to make it for you. We had a guy once who tried to break the phone receiver and use a jagged piece to commit suicide. I guess you'd better let us make the call for you. You just tell Harry Fleming who you want called and he'll do it for you."

I knew it wasn't any use. "Okay," I said. "Forget it."

"You see, boys," the Captain said, "he trusts us. He's got the right attitude. Now, what has Mr. March done?"

"Murder," Grant said.

You could see it wasn't any surprise to the Captain, although he tried to pretend it was.

"Not only that, Captain," Harry Fleming said, "but I think maybe he's one of them perverts. After he killed the girl, he took off all of her clothes."

"Took off her clothes, huh?" the Captain said. "What do you think he did to her?"

"He's an investigator," Grant said. "He must have been investigating."

"Nice work," Harry Fleming said. He licked his lips.

"What were you doing to the girl after she was dead?" the Captain asked me.

I sighed and tried once more. "Look," I said, "I know I'm probably old-fashioned, but don't you cops even show any interest in the report your coroner's going to make? Or isn't he going to make any?"

"Oh, the Coroner will report, all right," the captain said. "But by the time he gets it in, we'll probably have a confession and we can wrap the whole thing up."

"Not from me," I said. "I didn't kill the girl, but I had a chance to look at her a little before your two fly-cops came bouncing in. I know enough about it to know she hadn't been dead for more than two hours. I'm covered for those two hours. Well covered."

"An alibi?" the Captain said. "We'll have to discuss it."

"Okay," I said. "Bring on your lumps."

"You got us all wrong, March," the Captain said. "We don't do things like that in Aragon City. No rough stuff. We go in for psychology and all the new stuff. Why, would you believe it, the department spent thousands of dollars last year on new, up-to-date equipment for questioning prisoners."

"What did you buy?" I asked. "Hand-carved nightsticks?"

The Captain laughed. "You see, boys, he's got a sense of humor." He got up from the desk. "Okay, let's go."

"Where?" I asked.

"To another precinct," he said. "It gets a little crowded around here, and you might like a quieter place. Especially if you're going to tell what you did to that girl after you killed her."

So that was it. Precinct hopping. That way, even if someone found out that they'd pulled me in, no one would be able to find me until they were ready to have me found.

"Think we ought to put cuffs on him?" the Captain asked.

"Nah," Grant said, grinning. "He wouldn't try to run away."

He was right. I knew they'd like that. I might live through

what they were planning, but I certainly wouldn't if I did anything that looked like a break.

We went out of the station house and got into a police car. A few minutes later we pulled into the back of another precinct. We went inside.

The four of us entered a small room. There was only one tiny window and it was covered with bars. The walls were whitewashed, but they needed a new coat. There were finger-prints all over the walls and a few stains that looked like blood. There were several chairs in the room. There was a flexible light with a big bulb in it.

They shoved me into one of the chairs.

"Let me see," the Captain said. "Who'll question him first?"

"Me," Harry Fleming said. Eagerly.

The Captain nodded and the paunchy detective came over to stand in front of me. His right hand was in his pocket.

"There ain't no use," he said in that tired voice of his, "in wasting a lot of time talking. We ain't interested in a lot of fancy details. All we want you to do is confess that you killed the dame. Okay?"

I told him what he could go do to himself.

He grinned. "I like them tough," he said. "The tougher they are, the bigger the crack when they finally come apart." He wet his lips. Then he brought his right hand out of his pocket. He was holding what they call a soft blackjack. It was a nice long leather tube filled with sand. I knew the kind. It wouldn't cut any skin or leave any bruises that would last long. But when used by an expert it could give you a headache that would last for days. I had an idea that Harry Fleming was an expert.

"Anybody want to make me a bet?" he called back to the other two. "I'll bet he holds up for fifteen hours."

"He's not that tough," Grant said. "Remember the toughest guy we ever had in here was that nigger from San Diego. And he only went eleven hours. I don't think March can take it for more than ten hours at the outside."

"I'll go in the middle," the Captain said. "Twelve hours. You boys have both had a chance to look him over, so somewhere in between the two of you ought to be good."

"How much?" Fleming asked.

"Twenty bucks," said the Captain.

"Okay. Okay with you, Gene?"

"Okay," Grant said.

"Why don't you sell a few general admission tickets?" I asked. "Then you could make book and really clean up."

"Don't be impatient," Fleming said. "I'm coming to you." He reached up and tilted the light more directly into my face. "Look up at me, March."

I looked up at him, squinting my eyes against the light. I tried to look up and still keep my chin tucked in. I didn't quite make it.

He took a short, underhand swing and the blackjack caught me across the Adam's apple.

There was a knife of fire in my throat. I couldn't get my breath. I knew there was air around somewhere, but I just couldn't find it. I flopped around for a minute, then shoved my head down low. I started to come up, really pushing my lungs with the motion. A little air began to trickle in, cooling some of the fire.

He hit me over the head as I came up. I could feel the flash of pain all the way down to my chin. The pain was bright in the top of my head. Like a Fourth of July pinwheel.

"Those were just easy ones," Fleming said. His voice sounded like it was coming from a great distance. "You ain't going to disappoint me by folding already, are you?"

I had thought of something I wanted to call him. It was a fancy name, but I couldn't get it up past the fire in my throat. I could get my breath again, but it was still a four-alarm blaze. I couldn't get the word out, but he must have read it in my eyes, for he laid the sap against the side of my head the way Joltin' Joe leans wood against a fastball.* The room rocked.

After that, he really got down to work. The only sound in the room was the paunchy detective grunting as he swung, the almost silent swish of his arm through the air, the dull thwack of the sap against my head. Once in a while I'd grunt when it hit me, although I tried not to.

Harry Fleming was working up a sweat. He'd lost the tired glaze in his eyes and they were brightly feverish. His face was a little flushed. He kept wetting his lips and swallowing rapidly.

After a while there was so much ringing in my ears I could hardly hear the blows. They fell with a pulsing rhythm. The room had shrunk to a blazing, hurting light and the two of us. And our breathing. He was doing all the work, but I was breathing just as hard.

I'd started out by trying to count the blows, just to have

---

* Joe DiMaggio's last game was September 30, 1951, and he formally retired from baseball on December 11. *Hangman's Harvest* was published in February 1952, so the book was obviously written while he was still an active player.

something to think about. But somewhere along the way, I lost track. All sorts of thoughts floated through my head, only to be knocked out by one of his swings. I remembered the time I fell out of an apple tree and landed on my head when I was a kid. I remembered my first butch haircut. Once, when I looked up and caught a glimpse of the sweat running down Fleming's face, I remembered something Babe Dale had once said. She was a Denver madam. She was defending one of her girls who'd gotten mad at a customer and kicked him where it would hurt. "You'd be irritable too," she said, "if you had to work all night under a bunch of sweaty men." She was right. I was getting irritable and the night hadn't even started.

The rhythm of the blows picked up until it seemed that the sap was all over me. Then he swung a final blow that almost knocked me out of the chair.

He'd stopped hitting me, but it was some time before I could tell the difference. I could still feel the sap hitting my head, and once in a while I thought I could still hear it.

Harry Fleming stood limply in front of me. There were dark patches of sweat on his shirt and it clung to him. He was breathing so hard his body seemed to shudder every time he took a breath. The tired look was back in his eyes.

"The son of a bitch can take it," he said. His voice was thick and strained. "I'm really knocked out and he's still sitting there. I told you he was tough."

"You ought to take it easy, Harry," the Captain said. "We don't want you hurting yourself."

I made a couple of experimental noises and found out I

could talk. My voice sounded like I was in a tunnel. I told the three of them what I thought of them. I was using five-letter words because they were plurals. Then I threw in an eight-letter word and an eleven-letter word, just to dress it up. After that I quit. It wasn't worth the effort.

They looked at me like they were examining a footprint.

"Lots of life left in him," Grant said. "Maybe Harry's right. I don't remember the nigger feeling that good after the first session."

"He's going to make us work for it all right," Captain Logan said. He looked at his watch. "We've been here an hour. Let's go, boys. On your feet, March."

"Where?" I asked.

"To another precinct," the Captain said. He gave me a toothy grin. "Like I told you, we're scientific in Aragon City. We're making an experiment to see if different altitudes have anything to do with confessions."

He had a sense of humor like a rattlesnake.

I fished in my shirt pocket and got out the pack of cigarettes. They were getting a little soggy. I found a dry one and lit it. The smoke burned my throat more than usual.

"Uh-uh," I said. "It's your party. You want me to go to another precinct, you'll carry me."

"Okay," the Captain said. "But let's make it look real. Harry, Gene and I will hold him up; you give him a little ride on that sap."

"I'll walk," I said.

They looked disappointed.

I got to my feet. It made my head ring even more and the

walls tilted a little, but I made it. The four of us walked out and climbed into the police car.

The second precinct room looked just like the first one. This time a couple of local cops wandered in to watch the fun, but the Captain threw them out. I guess he didn't want any witnesses unless he was completely sure of them.

I walked over and sat in the chair under the big light without being told. I took a last drag on the cigarette and ground it out on the concrete floor. Then I braced myself in the chair and waited.

Nobody said anything. It was so quiet I could hear the Captain's watch ticking all the way across the room. I could almost hear the thumping that continued in my head like a delayed echo of the sap the paunchy detective had kept throwing against the side of my head.

A chair scraped on the floor and I felt my muscles jerk. They did it all by themselves without any thinking from me.

Grant dragged his chair across the floor and put it in front of me. He gave me a grin and pulled something from his pocket. It was a strange-looking contraption. Made out of metal, it looked something like an old-fashioned lantern. There were slits along the sides and the top was completely open. I could see something white inside. A leather thong was looped over the top.

"My own invention," Grant said proudly. He lit a match and thrust it through one of the slits. Flame curled up through the top opening. Then I could see the candle inside.

"Lift your head," Grant said. He slipped the leather thong over my head so that the contraption hung on my chest. It was warm on my chin, but not enough to burn.

"You got to hand it to Grant," the Captain said from across the room. "He's a cute one, all right."

That wasn't my word for Grant, but I let it pass.

"You see," Grant said to me, "as long as you hold your head up like that, the candle will keep your chin warm, but no more. But you try dropping your head a little and it'll raise a few blisters. Get the idea?"

I got it. I made an observation about his mother.

"You shouldn't talk like that," Grant said. "I'm doing it for your own good. Lots of guys, now, they'd just sit here and ask you questions and every time you tried lowering your head they'd belt you one on the chin. Rough stuff. But I don't go for that. This way, you and me can just talk natural-like and I don't have to get rough when you get lazy."

He made the thing complete then. He reached up and swung the light so it was directly in my eyes. I could either hold my head so the light would keep shining in my eyes or I could drop it and get burned. Some choice.

"Now, I'll tell you something, March," Grant said. "Harry Fleming is my partner and he's a swell guy. There ain't a better cop anywhere. But I got to admit that once in a while he gets a little rough. You know how it is. We go up to your place and we see this good-looking girl that you've murdered. Now, killing is bad enough, but then, after you knocked her off, you undressed her and God only knows what you did then. Me, I understand about those things. I know sometimes a guy gets a yen for something and he's got to have it come hell or high water. But Harry's different. He looks on women as something special, and when he saw how you had treated that little girl, he just got overexcited. You know how it is."

I knew how it was all right. But I said a short, hard word and let it go at that.

"Naturally, you're a little annoyed about it now," Grant continued, "but you'll get over it. Now, all we want from you, March, is a confession telling us how you killed the girl and why. That ain't so much to ask of you."

"Sure," I said. "That's all you want. What would you do with it? You know damn well it wouldn't hold up. Even if you switch barrels on my gun, you can't make the frame stick. I've got two perfect alibis covering the time."

"You probably have, at that," Grant said amiably. "Some guys have all the luck. But say we couldn't make it stick. You'd still be out of circulation for a while. And I got an idea you'd not do much work in Aragon City after that anyway."

I decided to try an experiment. I knew the answer already, but I might as well try it. "Okay," I said. "Call in a stenographer and I'll dictate a confession for you."

Grant cocked his head to one side and looked at me. "It don't sound right," he said. "You know, sometimes a guy will cook up a phony confession just for the fun of it. What do you think, Captain?"

"Might as well listen to him for a while," the Captain said cheerfully. "We don't want to call a stenographer in for nothing."

It went on like that. They weren't really interested in any of the answers I made, so I didn't bother making them. The first half hour wasn't so bad, but then the pains started shooting through my eyeballs, and my neck began to feel like a piece of wood that couldn't quite support my head.

Once I tried turning my head sideways to get away from the light but without burning my chin. Grant reached over with a cigarette and pressed the lighted end against my cheek. I jerked my head back, trying to squint against the light.

"Sorry," Grant said, but he was grinning. "My wife is always telling me that I'm too careless with my cigarettes."

There was a big difference between Grant's methods and those of Harry Fleming. Just offhand, most people might think Grant's way was easier to take. But it ended up about the same.

When Grant finished, pulling the leather thong over my head and stepping back, I sat there trying to will away the pain. Even after he turned off the light, I could still see it, and everything else in the room was a blur. My neck felt like it belonged to somebody else, but the pain was all mine. There was a burning from between my shoulder blades all the way to the top of my head. A burning, with a thousand little pricking pains like needles being thrust deeply into the flesh. I could feel a blister forming under my chin. Twice my head had sagged too low before I could whip my neck muscles back into service.

They led me out to the police car. I didn't pay much attention to the scenery, but after a short ride we arrived at another precinct. It looked like the first two. Maybe it was one of them. I didn't care. I dropped onto the chair they shoved under me and waited. I didn't bother trying to guess what was coming next.

It's a funny thing, getting worked over like this. I'd been beaten a couple of times before. When it happens, your sanity and your consciousness retreat to somewhere deep within you. The part of you that's important stays there, peering out from the distant caves that used to be your eyes. All of the pain is still there, all right, but it's not really with you. It's happening to someone else—someone who lives all around you. You feel it, but it doesn't touch you. And as long as you stay in there, you can take it. But if you ever creep out of that hidden cavern, if you ever reach out to live where the pain is … then you crack.

So I sat there, withdrawn within myself, watching the three cops. It was like looking at them through the wrong end of a telescope.

The Captain left the room. After a while he came back. He was carrying two things: A patrolman's nightstick, the light glinting from the polished wood, and a big white towel. He began wrapping the towel around the nightstick. He wrapped it carefully and with an air of affection. The Captain was another man who loved his work. "You young cops," he was saying to the other two, "are all right in your way, but sometimes you get the idea that you're smarter and more scientific than us old cops. But we can still show you a few things."

"You and Gene are alike," Harry Fleming said sourly. "You both talk too much."

"Now, Harry," the Captain said. He finished wrapping the nightstick against the palm of his hand. "You take this, now," he said. "I learned this from a doctor twenty-five years ago. It's real scientific. You just start whaling a man with a nightstick and you're liable to scatter his brains all over the place. A thing like that can start a scandal. But you wrap the nightstick up like this and it hurts just as much, but it don't leave any marks and it won't give a man a concussion—if you handle it right." He walked across the room to stand in front of me. "Milo March, the supersleuth," he said. There was a sneer in his voice. "You know, March, I think I'm going to tell you something. You won't remember it because I'm going to knock it right out of your head as soon as it gets in. You know who had Polly East send that broad out to see you last night?"

He waited for an answer, but I didn't bother giving him one. This was his day. From here on in, I wasn't going to do anything but make sure there was going to be another day.

"I did," he said. "I had the boys tail you and then give you just enough time so they could catch you."

He reached out and prodded me gently in the chest with the padded nightstick.

"That Mickie Gill was quite a piece, so that makes you either a fairy or pretty smart." He waited a minute, then added reluctantly, "I guess you were pretty smart. What kind of a pitch did you give the broad, March?"

I didn't say anything. I looked out at him and waited. "The broad kicked up a hell of a fuss with Polly," he said. "She let drop the idea that she might do some talking to you. Not that she could tell you anything important. But we don't like broads with long tongues. Not when they use them for talking."

He waited again. His face was beginning to get a little red. He was working himself up and getting a kick out of it.

"And we don't like smart out-of-town cops," he said. "There are a lot of guys around town, March, who would like to see you go home in a wooden box. They're big boys, too, and they could do it. But I figure my way is best." He looked me over some more.

"I know all about you, March," he said. "You've got a big reputation. You're a tough boy. Everybody knows all about it all over the country. They even wrote you up in a magazine once, telling how tough you are. Sure, you'll beat this murder rap. Maybe we'll never even charge you. But we got twenty-four hours before we have to book you. In that twenty-four hours, we're going to teach you that Aragon City is an unhealthy town. You're the cream of the crop, March. We're going to send you home begging for mercy. Maybe that'll make any other smart guys think twice before they get the idea they can come in and clean up Aragon City just like that."

He waited again, but this time you could tell he was all through talking. He was just getting set, letting anticipation swish around in his mouth before he took his first bite.

Then he laid the nightstick lovingly along the side of my head.

The padding over the wood kept it from hurting much where it hit. But inside of my head a little ball of fire exploded and the pain sprayed out all over.

The nightstick didn't make much noise when it hit. It was a sort of soft sound, almost lost in the grunt of effort the captain made when he swung. After a while, I could hear another sound. It was a sobbing breath that took a lot of effort to get it to its destination. I knew it was my breathing, but I didn't feel like I was doing it.

Finally he quit. Maybe because he was tired. I wouldn't know. It didn't seem any different when he quit except there was less noise. They led me out to the police car again.

After that, I lost count. Time sort of melted and slid together, like something painted by Salvador Dalí. Sometimes Harry Fleming was standing in front of me, then he'd seem to vanish and it would be Gene Grant or Captain Logan. Then we'd get in a car again and ride. Maybe they were taking me to different precincts; maybe they were just driving around the block and arriving back at the same one. It didn't make any difference.

Somewhere along the line, I was slumped in a chair trying to sort out the noises around me. There was a distant burring sound I couldn't place. Only after it stopped did I realize it was a phone.

I struggled a little with myself and things swung into focus. Not very clearly, but enough so I could make things out. The captain had picked up the phone. He was scowling.

"Yeah, this is Logan," he was saying. He listened and then he said, "Oh." That was all, but it was a different tone than I'd heard him use before. It sounded like Captain Logan was outranked. I pushed some of the pain out of the way and listened.

"Yeah," he was saying. "We're fixing it so the—" He broke off and listened. The phone receiver was crackling and he wasn't liking what he heard. "But—" he said, and then stopped to listen some more. "But—" he tried again, but it didn't take him very far. This time, when he finished listening, you could see he was all out of *but*'s.

"Okay, okay," he said. He hung up the phone.

"What's up, Sam?" Grant asked. He could read the signs as well as I could.

"Shut up," the Captain said savagely. He looked at me and there was hate in his eyes. "Get March out to the car."

This time we took a little longer ride. The windows were all open in the car and the wind was cool from the ocean. It revived me a little. Not much, but enough so that I began to feel like one big bruise.

We went into another precinct. This time we walked right past the little room in the back, up to the front. I recognized it as the same place they had first brought me. The same desk sergeant was on duty. He seemed to find something amusing about my face.

"So soon?" he asked the Captain. "The guy was hinged in the middle after all?"

"Shut up," the captain said. "Give the son of a bitch his stuff."

The desk sergeant looked surprised, but he didn't say anything. He got out a big manila envelope and began shoveling stuff across the desk to me. I put it in my pockets without looking at it. Finally, he pulled out my gun. Then he hesitated and looked at the captain.

"His gun too?" he asked.

"Yes," the captain bit off.

The sergeant looked at me again. Then he broke open the gun and took out the shells. He slipped the shells back in the envelope and handed me the gun. I jabbed it into the holster under my left arm.

"Okay, March," the Captain said. "Get to hell out of here. We're dropping the charge, but don't let me see you around again."

The two detectives stepped away from me. For the first time in what seemed like years, I was on my feet and on my own. I swayed a little, but I managed to stay there. I shuffled my feet enough to find out I could walk if I was careful.

"Okay," I said. It didn't sound like my voice. It sounded old and cracked. "If you see me, Captain, it'll only be after I've seen you first."

I made it through the door. Outside, I leaned against the building for a minute. I breathed deeply of the damp, cool air and my ribs hurt. I seemed to remember that once the Captain had used the padded nightstick on my side.

I fumbled in the pocket of my coat and finally found a pack of cigarettes. The package was crumpled and greasy to the touch. The cigarettes were all broken or sweat-stained a dirty brown color. I flung them from me and started down the steps.

A man came up the steps, almost running. He went past me, then stopped. It seemed that his hand touched my arm for a minute.

"March!" he said.

Milo March—that's you, a silent voice said inside me. Even so, I went down two more steps before I heard either voice. I turned and looked up at the man who stood two steps above me. The action of throwing my head back brought a new protest from the tight muscles of my neck. For a minute I could once more see the light beating into my eyes. I blinked against the remembered glare.

"March," the man said again. "Are you all right?"

The brightness faded from my eyes and I could see his face. It was familiar. This was someone I knew—it seemed like someone I had known a long time before. I picked through my memory, through the part that went back farther than the bright lights and the three cops. It was Yale. Martin Yale. The District Attorney.

"Yeah," I said. "I'm all right."

He came down the two steps and grabbed my arm. He peered into my face. "Good heavens, man," he said. "They beat you up, didn't they?"

"Yeah," I said.

"Who did it? Logan?"

"Logan," I said. It was a sharp memory, the kind you can taste. It had a bitter taste. I'd remember it for a long time. "Logan and Fleming and Grant."

"Come on," he said. "I'll get you to a hospital." He pushed at my arm.

I shook his hand loose. I couldn't stand the pressure. Even my clothes pressed too much.

"No," I said. "No hospital."

"But you've got to. You may be hurt. Bad."

"I'm hurt," I said and the admission made it worse. "But those boys are experts. I'll live. At least, long enough. ... What were you doing here?"

"Looking for you," he said.

"Why?"

"Good God, man," he said. He sounded angry. "I just found out you'd been arrested. I know these bastards. I wanted to get you out."

"You phone?" I asked him.

"No."

I thought it over. The thinking went a little better, but the road was still bumpy. "How'd you know I was arrested?"

"I went over to your apartment about thirty minutes ago," he said. "Your door was unlocked and the place looked like a steamroller had gone through it. I talked to one of your neighbors and they told me about you going away with two men. The description sounded like Grant and Fleming."

"There was a dead girl there," I told him. "Earlier. They killed her. But that was the excuse for dragging me in."

He swore. "They didn't book you?" he asked.

"No," I said. I managed a grin. "They'll probably send you a nice, pretty report when they get around to it. Person or persons unknown."

"Okay," the D.A. said. "Let's go to the hospital whether you want to or not. I want a doctor to examine you. Maybe we can pin something on the three of them."

I started to shake my head, but it hurt too much. "No," I said.

"Why not? I thought you wanted to clean up the town."

"My way," I said. "You're a big boy, Yale. You ought to know all about police brutality cases. They never get anywhere. We're going to get them where it hurts or not at all. You just forget all about it."

"Okay," he said, but he didn't like it. "What do you want to do?"

"Give me a cigarette," I said.

He stuck a cigarette in my face and lit it. I drew deeply and it revived me a little more.

"What time is it?" I asked. I really didn't care. I was just curious.

"Ten o'clock," he said.

Seven hours. They had worked over me for seven hours. I couldn't help feeling a little good about that. It was a new record for me.

"Take me home," I said. "Only don't drive over any rough streets. I bruise easily."

He swore again. But he drove me home without any more talk.

FIVE

I made it up the stairs and went into my apartment. The room looked a little messy. A fussy housekeeper might have been upset. But I didn't pay any attention. I went into the kitchen. The brandy was still there. I poured a water glass full. Then I drained it in long, steady swallows. I leaned against the stove and waited for it to start working.

It built a small fire in my stomach and fanned out. It took my mind away from the rest of my body. I went over and scrounged around in the cracker box on the table. My spare gun was still there. I put the crackers back over it and left it.

I went into the bathroom. After the brandy, I thought I could face a mirror. I leaned over and took a look.

It was my face all right, only it looked different. The skin was drawn tight over my cheekbones. My lips were clamped together like the shell of a clam. I made the muscles relax, feeling the soreness ripple up through my face. There was a blister about the size of a quarter under my chin. There was another, smaller blister on one cheek. Here and there were a few light bruises, but they'd go away quickly enough. I was right about the three cops. They were experts.

I turned on the shower and stripped. There were a few bruises around my shoulders and sides, but they were light too. By morning there wouldn't be a mark on me except the burns. But the soreness and the headache would be with me for days.

When the water was running as hot as I could stand it, I got under the shower. I stayed there, letting the water run over me until the hot water was gone. Then I got out and toweled myself gingerly. The hot water had taken a little of the stiffness out of my muscles. I looked in the mirror again. I needed a shave, but to hell with it. My face was too sore.

I got another glass of brandy in the kitchen. I washed down a small handful of aspirin and went into the living room. I sat on the edge of the bed and worked slowly on the rest of the brandy.

After a while I was feeling no pain. I rolled over on the bed and went to sleep.

It was two o'clock in the afternoon when I awakened. Technically it was the next day, but I was hardly aware of it. The hours of the night before had melted and run together so that I couldn't have sworn whether it was the same day or the same year. But I knew that I still ached. My head thumped and there was a strange ringing in my ears. After a while I realized it was the phone. To hell with it, too. I let it ring.

My mouth tasted like an old sweatshirt. I went into the kitchen, turning off the lights I'd left on when I went to sleep. There was some orange juice in the refrigerator next to the ice cubes. I couldn't taste much, but it was cold and it felt good going down. The phone stopped ringing, which helped some.

I thought of making some eggs, but then I thought to hell with it. I went back into the living room.

The phone starting ringing again. I picked up the receiver

and put it down on the table. A faint squawking came from it, but that didn't bother me any.

I stretched out on the bed and lit a cigarette. My back was so sore I could feel every individual feather in the mattress. The cigarette didn't taste so good either, so I put it out.

I think I slept some more, but never very soundly. Once someone hammered on the door, but after a time they gave it up and left. I remember noticing the clock a couple of times. Once it was three-thirty and the second time it was five.

It was dark when I came awake again. My head still hurt, but for the first time I was hungry. I got up and turned on the lights. It was seven o'clock.

The eggs tasted fine. Five of them. I wolfed them down and then polished off the bottle of milk. I still hurt just as much, but I was beginning to feel that I'd live. All I needed to make it complete was some brandy, but the bottle was empty.

I went into the bathroom and took another shower. Then I had enough courage to try shaving. Part of the time it felt like I was cutting my own throat, but I made it.

Something about the session with the three cops kept nagging at my memory. It kept gnawing around the edge, but I couldn't get it any closer. Every time I started thinking about the details, I'd start feeling the blows all over again and my mind would jump away from it like a frightened dog. I knew there was something important that I should remember, if I could only dredge it up. Finally I said to hell with that, too.

I got dressed and then I dug some fresh shells out of my suitcase and slipped them into my gun. I went back to the bathroom and stuck a couple of Band-Aids on my face. A small one on my cheek and a bigger one under my chin. Then I went downstairs and got into the Cadillac.

I wasn't going any place in particular. But I wanted to get away from myself. I couldn't sleep anymore and I didn't feel ready for action. I wanted to see how much brandy I could drink and how far I could get away from the memory of anything that had happened during the last twenty-four hours. Later, when it had all been washed a little cleaner in alcohol, I'd come back and look it square in the face. Maybe then I could pick up a few pieces. But not now.

I drove over to the main part of town and started cruising down Wilson Boulevard. I passed a lot of little joints and bistros, but they all looked cozy and intimate. That wasn't what I wanted. Not then. I wanted lights—not too bright. And people—not too bright either. Finally I came to a place that looked about right. It was big. It was fancy. There was a sign that announced the Cassandra Club. I parked in the back and went in.

It was right. There were a lot of tables, mostly full. There was a good orchestra working away at some pretty good music. There was the right kind of waiters, with the right kind of headwaiter who looked down his nose in just the right way. There was plenty of noise, but it wasn't too loud. There was a big bar and even there you could spot a generous sprinkling of bare backs outlined by the wisps of evening gowns.

I stood inside for a minute, drinking it all in. I fended off the headwaiter with a wiggle of my eyebrows and looked around. I caught something that looked familiar and took another look at one of the tables. There were several people there, and one of them was the redhead from the reception room of the Committee. She was wearing some kind of green dress that really did things for her.

She saw me and waved. I waved back and headed for the bar. She was something I wanted, all right, but I wasn't in the mood. I figured she'd keep. Things that nice don't spoil overnight.

I climbed on a stool at the bar and looked for the bartender. One came trotting over.

"Brandy," I said. "The best you've got." What I'd had in the apartment was already wearing off, and my aches were coming back in full force.

"Shot or pony?" he asked.

"Pony, hell," I said, "I want the whole horse. Bring me a bottle and a glass. You can add a small glass of water on the side if it'll make you happy, but don't go out of your way."

He looked at me and went away. I grinned. It always happens like that. There's an old superstition that brandy drinkers don't live long and bartenders, are always looking at me as if I had one foot in the grave. As a matter of fact sometimes I did, but not from brandy.

The bartender brought the bottle and the glasses. He looked as if he wanted to make a speech, but he took my money and went away. I started working on the brandy.

Somebody climbed on the stool next to me, but I didn't look around. I wanted to have people around me all right, but not too close around. I kept on nibbling at the brandy and minding my own business. I was beginning to get a glow and I wanted to nurse it into a major project.

Some perfume drifted along the bar and competed with the brandy fumes. The perfume was familiar. Maybe if I concentrated on it, I could get all the answers without looking around. Just like Sherlock Holmes. But I thought to hell with it. Everything I wanted was in the bottle in front of me.

"Hello, Milo," she said.

I looked around. She was wearing an evening gown. Black instead of red this time. The same plunging neckline. Mink wrap instead of stole. The same careful blond hair. The movie star, hot one night and a brush-off the next morning. The one I'd started to wonder about.

"Hello," I said.

"Aren't you going to buy me a drink?" she asked.

I'd already finished the water in the one glass. I pushed the glass and the bottle of brandy in her direction. She splashed some brandy in the glass and drank it neat. I liked her for that. She set the glass down and looked at me.

"What happened to you, Milo?" she asked. She reached out and touched my cheek near the small Band-Aid. Her fingers were soft and cool.

"I cut myself on a sharp cop," I said.

She laughed lightly. She leaned over and took my face between her hands. Her eyes were searching. She was breathing a little faster.

I submitted in a detached sort of way, gazing down at the plunging neckline. It didn't leave much to the imagination, but then I didn't have to imagine. I could still remember that much. Her perfume drifted up to tug at my senses. But I was still more interested in my brandy.

"Poor Milo," she said. She leaned back and looked at me. There were color spots in her cheeks. "There are little bruises all over your face. Were you beaten up terribly?"

"Not at all," I said politely. "It was merely a typographical error."

She laughed again. "Is that why you're so unfriendly?"

"I'm not unfriendly," I said. "It's just that I'm delicate. If people get too close to me, I bruise." I looked at her and remembered what I wanted to know. "Tell me something, Vega," I said.

"Of course, darling."

"The other night," I said, "night before last, when you picked me up in that saloon. You remember?"

She laughed. "I'm afraid I was pretty high," she said. "I don't usually do things like that, Milo. I'm afraid the whole thing is sort of vague in my mind. I passed out later, didn't I?"

"Not too far," I said. "But, look, honey—I don't believe in accidents. I came to Aragon City a day before anyone expected me. I meet you in a saloon. Then I find out you're on the Committee that's hiring me, and you don't seem very surprised when I turn out to be the guy they're hiring. So how come we met in that bar?"

Her eyes went wide, in as phony a look as I ever saw. "Why, Milo," she said, "I was just there and you just happened to come in. We looked at each other and it was romance."

I said the first thing that came in my mind and it made even her wince. "If," I added, "you had lines like those in your pictures, you'd be back in Keokuk slinging hash. Now, let's start all over again. This time, play it the way it was written. Okay?"

"Okay," she said lightly. "It's really pretty simple, Milo. I happened to be at the airport when you came in. I recognized you. I knew you weren't supposed to arrive until the next day, so I was curious. I followed you. When I saw you were going in a straight line, stopping in every bar you came to, I merely went ahead and waited for you to arrive."

"Uh-huh," I said. "How come you recognized me?"

"When the Committee first talked about hiring you, I was curious enough to find out more about you. I found an old magazine with an article about you and there was a picture too. You sounded like an—well, an exciting person, and I wanted to meet you. So I did."

"Uh-huh," I said. I drank some more brandy and thought it over. It sounded all right, but there was still something about her that was off key.

"Milo," she said. She leaned forward and put one hand on my arm. "Let's leave and go to my place. I want to hear all about whoever beat you up. I want to hear everything about it." Her eyes were shining and she was breathing so fast the plunging neckline was really plunging.

Then I got it. I should have seen it before.

"Aren't you with some people?" I asked carefully.

"Oh, them," she said. It was a dismissal. "It's you I'm interested in, Milo. I want to know what happened. I'll take care of you, Milo. I'll make you feel better."

"I've got an idea that you'd make me feel worse," I said deliberately. "I've been wondering about you, Vega. Now I'm getting it. The other night when you passed out, it was strictly phony, wasn't it?"

"Why do you talk so much?" she asked. "We had fun, didn't we?"

"Did we?" I said evenly. "I'm getting the picture now, Vega. You read an article about me and you figured I was a real tough boy. A guy who shot people and got shot sometimes maybe I'd even killed somebody once. So you made a pickup. Then when you knew for sure I was going to take you, you pulled a pass-out so I'd have to do it with a little violence. I remember now, you looked real excited when there was almost a fight in that bar. Then tonight you see I look like maybe I've been beaten up, so right away you start getting sexy again. That's what you get your kicks from—from violence, not the real thing."

It was a long speech, so I took a drink. Then I looked at her.

Her face was pale and her mouth had tightened. But the glint was still in her eyes. Maybe even brighter. She was thinking I was getting rough and she liked it.

Right then I wasn't feeling very friendly toward anything in human form. And even at my best, I didn't like my women that kinky. I laughed.

"What's so funny?" she asked. Her voice was a little husky.

"I've seen those pinup pictures of you your studio had made up for the GIs," I said. "A lot of them go to civilians too. There's a name for guys who collect cheesecake pictures like that, and in your own way you're no better than they are."

"You son of a bitch," she said. She meant it too. Her face was white and pinched.

"So I'm a son of a bitch," I said amiably. "I've been called worse things in the past few hours. Look, honey, under the circumstances, you were okay as a one-night stand. But that doesn't mean that we're old friends. It doesn't even mean that I want a return engagement. Now, why don't you run back to your friends and leave me alone with my brandy?"

She told me what I could do with my brandy. I'd never heard her talk like that before, and I might have winced, but I knew it would hurt. She turned around and started to walk away, walking stiff-legged the way some women do when they're mad. It gave a funny little flounce to her hips.

I almost called her back to say I was sorry. I knew I'd been pretty rough on her, that I was working off some of the venom I felt toward three cops. But then I thought to hell with it. I went back to work on the brandy.

When I got the bottle down to where it was only about a third full, I suddenly realized I was feeling fine. There was a fine coating of alcohol between my nerve ends and most of my bruises. Even my headache had retreated until it didn't bother me too much. I went back to drinking the brandy for its own sake rather than its medicinal value. It was good brandy.

Sometime while I was finding out that I felt pretty good, somebody slipped onto the stool next to me. At first I thought Vega Russell was back, but then I caught a whiff of perfume and knew I was wrong. This was a fresh scent, not that bottled mating call that Vega wore.

I was having a little debate with myself. Should I look or shouldn't I? Not that I felt any more like romance than I had earlier, but I was more mellow and there was always the chance I might enjoy just looking. It seemed like a weighty problem. I gave it my full attention.

"Mr. March ... ," a voice said. So I looked.

She was young, maybe no more than nineteen or twenty. She had a pretty face, framed with tight curls of black hair. It wasn't the conventional pretty face, but I liked it. Her eyes were gray. From the expression in them, I guessed she was fairly high.

"Hello," I said when I'd finished looking.

"I thought she was never going to leave, and I wanted to talk to you," she said.

"Who?" I asked.

"That Vega Russell," she said. She pouted a little when she said it.

"That's right, she was here, wasn't she?" I said solemnly. "But now she's gone and you're here."

She gave me an uncertain smile—like she wasn't sure whether she might want to take it back.

"Mr. March," she said, "are you here to investigate my father?"

"I don't know," I said honestly. "Do I know your father? And if so, how come I don't know you?"

"I'm Janet Marshall," she said. "My father is Sherman Marshall, the Commissioner of Parks."

I remembered her father then. He was the member of the Committee who looked and sounded like a politician. The one who hoped to become mayor. I remembered discussing him with Miss Saxon, too. I'd told her that the guy who was the crook in the present administration might like to be on her Committee.

"Why do you ask, Janet?" I asked her.

"Why, everybody knows you're here to investigate the city officials," she said.

I sighed. "Everybody?"

She gave her shoulders an impatient little twist. "Well, everybody knows there is an investigation. I guess everybody doesn't know that you're doing it. But I heard Father mention your name, so I knew."

"As a matter of fact," I said, "practically everybody does know it's me. If anyone has been left out of the secret, you can be sure they're unimportant. ... But how did you know where to find me?"

"I was sitting at the same table with Vega Russell and her crowd. I heard her mention your name."

"I bet it was a four-star mention," I said. "Did she know you were coming over to see me?"

She nodded.

"What did she say about that?"

Her face colored a little. "She made a vulgar remark," she said. "I guess she was angry with you."

"What did she say?"

The girl's color got a little higher.

"Come on," I said. "I'm a big boy and I promise I won't blush."

"It really wasn't much," she said. "She—she merely wanted to know if I was wearing a tear-proof girdle."

"Well, are you?" I asked.

Up to then, she'd been pretty much the big little girl, tying a bun on. But then she did one of those sudden changes young girls do sometimes, and suddenly sounded older than her years.

"A good detective should know without asking," she said. The look that went with it was older and wiser too.

"You're so right," I said. "What did you want to talk to me about?"

"My father," she said. "You haven't told me whether you're investigating him or not."

"I really don't know," I said. "You've been reading too many books, honey. I don't go around looking for clues. I just sit around, sometimes drinking as much brandy as I can, and let things drift in my direction. Whatever comes to me, I investigate."

"All right, I've come to you," she said. Before I could decide how she meant that, she went on. "I want to talk to you about my father. For the record." She said this last solemnly, like it made it official or something.

I sighed again. I didn't want to do any work. I wanted to get drunk enough to forget work. Besides, I didn't think she could tell me anything. But she wasn't going to give up that easily.

"Okay, talk," I said.

"Not here," she said. "Someone might hear me. Don't you have a car?"

"I have a car," I said. I looked at the bottle in front of me. Then I put the bottle in my side pocket and climbed off the stool. I saw the dirty look the bartender gave me, but I thought to hell with that too. I'd paid for the bottle and I wasn't going to leave it to the help. "Come on," I said to the girl.

She slid off the stool and I looked at the rest of her. It was nice. And she wasn't wearing a girdle either. Her hips were round and firm, neither flattened by a girdle nor blurred by age. I looked up to see her watching me and I grinned.

"So you're not wearing one," I said. "You see, I'm a good detective after all. With no hands, too."

She gave me a look from beneath her eyelashes and we started for the door.

"Tell me," she said, "did you sleep with Vega Russell?" She surprised me for a minute with that one.

"A smart woman should know without asking," I said brightly.

"I just wanted to see what you'd say," she said. "I wonder if there's a man around that hasn't slept with her." She sounded bitter. I guessed that she must have lost a boyfriend to the movie star.

"Honey," I said, "Vega Russell is like smoking opium or sitting in poison ivy. It's something a guy has to do once if he gets the chance. But there'd have to be something wrong with a guy who let it become a habit."

We climbed into the Cadillac and I looked at her. "Where will we go to talk?" I asked her.

"Why not your apartment?" she wanted to know.

"Why not?" I said.

I drove down Wilson and then cut over to Miramar Terrace. It was only a ten-minute drive and neither of us talked on the way. I parked in front of the house and we walked in.

I remembered that I was always liable to have visitors, so I opened the door and stepped in first. I turned on the light. The apartment looked the same as when I left it, so I stepped aside for her.

I closed the door and turned to look at her. She came into my arms and her mouth found mine the way a hummingbird goes for a flower.

Her mouth was warm and soft, and all it was doing was giving. Her body pressed against me. Even through my coat, I could feel her hard young breasts.

I'd started out thinking I wasn't interested in romance in any of its forms. All I wanted was a bottle of brandy and the amnesia it could buy me. I didn't want anything pressing against me, not even warm flesh.

She changed my mind with that one kiss.

Afterward, I reached across her to the stand and got two cigarettes. I lit them and stuck one in her mouth. She didn't say anything, but she took it.

I leaned back, propping my head up with one hand, and looked at her. It was the first good look I'd taken. Before, my blood was pounding too hard.

She had the kind of body that only a very young girl has. It was hard and soft at the same time. It was a nice body—not the kind of ripe, beautiful body a woman should have, but the promise of the ripeness was there. And she had the kind of quick, savage fire that goes with the youngness. The kind of fire to burn yourself in, but never to slowly warm yourself in.

She opened her eyes and saw me looking at her. She gave me a slow smile.

"Was I better than Vega Russell?" she asked.

"Honey, that's a hell of a question," I said. I saw that didn't satisfy her, so I thought about an answer. "You can't answer questions like that with a yes or no," I said. "You're different, Janet. Different, and fresher, and healthier."

We were silent some more, then she turned toward me with a quick gesture.

"You want to find the man who protects crime in Aragon City, don't you?" she asked. "The man who protects gangsters and takes their money?"

"Yes," I said. I didn't want to talk about it. I wasn't sure why, but I knew that I didn't. But I could see we were going to talk about it.

"I think it's my father," she said. She looked at me with wide, frightened eyes. "Is that a terrible thing to say?"

"I don't know," I said honestly. "Is it?"

"But I have to tell the truth," she said. "I couldn't live with myself if I didn't. You can see that, can't you?"

I ducked my head to light another cigarette from the first one. Maybe she took the movement for a nod, because she went on.

"If I lied to protect my father, then I'd be as bad as he is," she said. "It'll hurt me, and my mother, if he's caught, but it might hurt worse to live with it in here." She touched one of her breasts in an almost childish gesture.

"What makes you think it's your father?" I asked.

She told me all she knew about her father. She knew plenty, even though it didn't mean much to me. She knew about him and Vega Russell. She knew about a mistress he kept down in Hollywood. She knew about him going to Polly East's. She knew about his drinking and gambling. She even knew about his pulling a little fast one with city money in the purchase of ground for a new city park. It all added up to a picture of a pretty unpleasant man, but didn't give me anything except a worse taste in my mouth. There were a lot of unpleasant people in town, and they weren't all giving protection to Johnny Doll and Jan Lomer.

When she finished, she cried. I held her close and stroked her hair until she ran out of sobs. Neither of us talked for a while.

"Will you arrest my father?" she finally asked.

I shook my head. "Honey," I said, "I'm not going to arrest anybody. All I have to do is get proof that somebody in Aragon City is taking money for a fix. Whoever it is, he's spreading the money around in a lot of places, mostly among cops. But some of the other city officials will be involved too. Maybe your father is one of them and maybe he isn't. But my job is to get the top guy. Once I get him, the roof will cave in. The D.A. can get court orders to go into the bank accounts and bank boxes of everybody, and he can clean up all the small fry. He could do that right now. But it's no good without the top guy. Even if the top man is Sherman Marshall, you haven't given me anything that would be proof for the Committee. It has to be proof that will stand up in court."

"I'll get it," she said. She turned toward me and threw one arm over me. Her fingers played with my chest. "I'll get it for you. I'll watch him all the time and give you reports. We can meet—like this—in your apartment, and no one will know. Every night, if you'd like …"

I removed her arm gently and got up. I walked over and got the bottle of brandy I'd brought from the club. My head was starting to hurt again. I took a long drink. "Want some?" I asked her.

She shook her head, her black curls bouncing on the pillow. "I don't need it," she said. "Not when you've—just brought me to life."

It sounded like a line out of a bad novel. I took another drink so I wouldn't have to answer.

"Okay, honey," I said. "Let's get dressed. It's getting late."

I dressed quickly and went into the bathroom. I looked at myself in the mirror. I didn't look any better. In fact, I looked worse. And the bruises were a pale yellow.

When I went back to the other room, she was dressed. She was just finishing with a new mouth, using a small hand mirror.

"Let's go, honey," I said. "You want me to take you home?"

"I have my own car," she said. "At the club."

We went downstairs and I drove back to the Cassandra Club on Wilson Boulevard. I parked the Cadillac and walked her over to her car. It was a new Ford convertible. I helped her in. Then I leaned over and kissed her on the cheek.

"I'll call you, Janet," I said. "You just take it easy until you hear from me."

She gave me another one of those looks from beneath her eyelashes. "I'll be waiting," she said.

She started the motor and put it in gear. She looked at me and her eyes were big again.

"Good night, Mr. March," she said. She drove off.

I'd been playing around with the truth ever since we were lying on the bed smoking the cigarettes. Now it hit me. And hard. It was the "Mr. March" that did it. I stood there in front of the nightclub and shivered. I felt dirty, deep inside where you couldn't reach it to scrub away the dirt.

I'd known even when I was taking her that I was holding a hard burst of fire that was more than passion. I'd known there was something wrong about her attitude toward Vega Russell. I'd thought it had to do with a boyfriend. I'd been right and wrong on that one. I'd known there was something off balance about the way she talked of her father. Everything had been there, but I just hadn't stopped to read it. Too many lumps on the head and too many ponies in my stomach had helped me to kid myself. Now I was taking a good look.

I thought of that old line "I'll hate myself in the morning" and grinned. I wouldn't have to wait until morning.

I'm not one of those guys who buy psychology right down the line, but I'd rubbed around enough to know there was something in it. Enough to know that Janet Marshall was a girl who hated her father like poison and thought she'd just jabbed a big nail in his tire. But more than that—she was also a girl who loved her father even while she hated him. On some level of her mind, she'd always wanted to go to bed with him. And for twenty minutes or so I'd been her father.

"Good night, Mr. March," I muttered to myself, and went into the club.

Most of the tables were empty by this time, and there were only a few stragglers left at the bar. I noticed that Vega Russell was no longer in the club. Neither was the redhead from the Committee office.

I was halfway to the bar when I got hit by another delayed reaction. The night before—some twenty-nine hours earlier—I'd had a date with Betty Carr, the redhead. I'd been supposed to meet her at seven-thirty. In the Cassandra Club. This club. At seven-thirty, it was true, I'd been busy with a different sort of club. But then, when I did show up—only twenty-four hours late—she was sitting there. Maybe still looking for me. She'd waved to me. And I'd waved back and that was all.

I said a hard word, a Hemingway word, to myself and went on to the bar. It was one o'clock in the morning. If I concentrated on only the one thing, I just had time to get drunk before closing time.

I made it.

SIX

It was a hell of a morning. I knew that even before I was awake. I hurt from my feet right on up. The muscles of my legs were sore from tension. But the upper half of me was sore from the drubbing the three cops had given me. And I mean sore. It even hurt to breathe. My head felt sore inside and out. And it was further complicated by a hangover. A grandfather of a hangover. A hangover on wheels.

I groaned and put off opening my eyes. I was afraid that the light—just plain ordinary daylight—would put the finishing touches to me and I'd pop open like an expired clam.

From somewhere there was the smell of coffee. I wanted some more than anything I could think of, but I hated to think of getting up to make it. I could even hear the rattle of cups and saucers as plainly as if it were in my own kitchen.

Then I forgot some of my headache, because it *was* coming from my own kitchen.

Still not opening my eyes, I inched my hand in under my pillow. I couldn't remember if I'd been too drunk to put my gun there when I went to bed. I hadn't, and that made me feel better.

I pulled the gun out, rolled over facing the kitchen, and opened my eyes all with one movement. There was nobody in sight, but I was ready.

Betty Carr came through the door. She was wearing a green knit dress that made her look like a million dollars—in cash. But what looked even better was the cup of coffee she was carrying in her hand.

"Good morning, Hopalong,"* she said. "Expecting a few cattle rustlers this morning?"

I grinned and shoved the gun back under the pillow. I looked to see if the sheet was still covering me. It was. "No danger of rustlers around here," I said. "All I ever get are bum steers."

"Relatively speaking," she said, "you're pretty bright this morning. Better than I expected. Here." She held out her hand and there were three aspirins in it. I took them. Then she handed me the coffee.

I put the aspirins in my mouth and took a swallow of coffee. Then I took another sip of the coffee. She'd made it just right. Strong. And black. It even had the right amount of sugar in it. And there was also a generous lacing of brandy.

"It's wonderful," I said. "You're wonderful. When will you marry me?"

"Not before breakfast."

I looked at her and she seemed as fresh as a morning breeze right off the ocean. I found myself wishing that I were all dressed up in my best, instead of lying in bed with a hangover and bleary eyes. In some peculiar fashion, that made me think of Vega Russell and Janet Marshall, and I was ashamed of myself. Especially that I'd stood this girl up for a dose of father fixation.

---

* Thanks to the TV series bearing his name, the fictional cowboy Hopalong Cassidy was at the height of his fame at the time *Hangman's Harvest* was published (1952).

"I'm a bastard," I said.

"I know," she said solemnly. "But you are a rather nice one at that."

"I mean it," I insisted. "I'm sorry I stood you up night before last. There couldn't be a good reason for standing you up— but I've got as good a one as is possible."

"Did I ask you?"

"But I want to tell you," I said. "The cops picked me up in the afternoon. From three until ten at night, they were working over me. But good. That was why I didn't show up when I was supposed to, and why I still didn't remember when I did show up twenty-four hours later."

I could see she was looking at the two Band-Aids on my face and the bruises. There was sympathy on her face, but not too much of it. It was as if she guessed that I didn't want anyone cooing over my broken head.

"It's okay, Milo," she said. "I thought something like that must have happened when I saw you last night. You looked punchy. Now, drink your coffee."

I drank the coffee and appreciated her. This was the kind of woman I could love.

When I'd finished the coffee, she brought me a second cup. By the time I was halfway through that, I began to feel more human. My head was better, although the real headache wouldn't go away for days. I'd been beaten over the head before, and I knew. But my hangover was practically gone and I was beginning to feel like functioning again.

"What time is it?" I asked.

"Ten o'clock."

"Wait a minute," I said. "What are you doing here if it's ten o'clock? Won't you lose your job?"

She shook her head. "I phoned Mr. Willis at his office and told him I'd be late. It doesn't make any difference. The Committee is having a meeting right after lunch, but there won't be anyone in before then."

"One more thing," I said. "How did you get in here? People are starting to walk in and out of my apartment like it was Union Station."

"It was easy for me," she said. "I've been Mr. Willis's secretary for a long time. You remember he owns this building? So all I had to do was pick up a master key from the superintendent of the building. That was all."

"Why?" I asked.

"What do you mean?" she asked. She was stalling and we both knew it.

"Why?" I asked again. "Why did you do it for a guy who stood you up on his first date?"

"Let's say it's part of my job," she said lightly. "I get paid for looking after the Committee. You work for the Committee, so I look after you too."

I thought it over and shook my head. "I won't buy that," I said. "It's got holes in it. Try again."

"I don't know, Milo," she said. "I knew you wouldn't just forget we had a date. I was sure something had happened. Then I knew it when I saw you walk into the club last night. I guessed that you might have been beaten up. I wanted to go over to you, but I think I knew how you felt. I knew you were probably going to get drunk, and that later you'd remember we had a date and that you'd probably feel terrible this morning. And—here I am.

It sounded right, even though I didn't know many people like that. I started to say so, but she stopped me.

"Don't say it," she said. She gave me a smile and took the coffee cup. "Stay right there for a minute. There's more to the Carr cure."

"I can already tell you it's better than the Keeley Cure," I said.

She laughed and went into the kitchen. Then I heard her go into the bathroom. When she came back, she was carrying a bottle. It didn't look like a brandy bottle.

"This is alcohol," she said like she was giving a lecture. "But not the kind you're familiar with, Mr. March. This is the kind of alcohol you should have tried in the first place."

She sat on the edge of the bed and splashed the rubbing alcohol over my arms and shoulders. She rubbed vigorously. Later she put some on my face and head. Her hands were firm but tender. Her touch was almost as good a medicine as the alcohol.

"There," she said when she'd finished. She stood up and smiled at me. "You go get dressed while I make some breakfast. Bacon and eggs all right?"

"Right now," I said fervently, "you could feed me fried paper and make me think it was ambrosia."

She laughed and went into the kitchen.

I got up and took my clothes into the bathroom. I shaved, lingered under the shower, and finally got dressed. I even had a couple of ideas while I was getting dressed.

When I came out of the police station that night, I knew that something had happened which had some special meaning for me, but I couldn't pin it down. Every time I'd tried thinking about it the night before, my mind had veered away like a skittish colt. But suddenly, under the shower that morning, I knew what it was.

Captain Logan was the link. He was the first step to the man I wanted to find. If I was right, he was probably the only step to the man on top.

I left the bathroom and walked to the kitchen door. The strips of bacon were draining on paper on the top of the stove. She was cooking the eggs, but she looked up as I stopped in the doorway.

"Breakfast will be ready in a minute," she said. She looked me over and gave an imitation wolf whistle.

"Thanks for the vote of confidence," I said. "I'll be right in."

I turned and walked out the front door. I went quietly so she wouldn't ask questions. It wasn't that I didn't trust her, but I was beginning to work out an idea, and the fewer people who knew the details the better. The rough idea, I might tell her.

I walked quickly down the stairs and climbed into the Cadillac. I started the motor and drove around the corner. I parked the car and went back upstairs. It had taken only a couple of minutes, and I could hear her dishing out the eggs.

The phone started to ring.

"Milo," she called from the kitchen.

"I'll get it," I said.

"Tell whoever it is to make it short," she called. "Unless you want to eat cold eggs."

I picked up the phone and said hello. It was Martin Yale, the District Attorney.

"How are you feeling, March?" he wanted to know.

"Better," I said. "There'll be a few things to remind me of our friends for several days, but I feel much better. What's on your mind?"

"You," he said. "I think you're wrong about not pressing charges. There might be a weak link and that would make it snap."

"No," I said firmly. "There's only one link in this chain that's any good, and it's not a weak one. But you can do one thing for me, Yale."

"What's that?"

"I want to know Captain Logan's complete schedule for today," I said, lowering my voice. "Then, after you've gotten it for me, forget I asked you."

"Okay," he said. "Call me back in about an hour. Or I'll call you."

"I'll call," I said, and hung up. I went into the kitchen.

The kitchen had one of those breakfast nooks, and she had everything set up there. The eggs looked wonderful, and I realized I was hungry. I sat down. She was already sitting across from me.

"What about you?" I asked. "No breakfast?"

"I've already had breakfast," she said. "I'm joining you in coffee, though." She indicated her cup.

I went to work on the bacon and eggs. She was quiet while I ate. Finally I finished and leaned back, stirring my coffee. I grinned at her.

"Thanks, honey," I said.

"Think nothing of it," she said. "We like to make visitors feel at home in Aragon City. It's just part of the service."

"It more than makes up for the official service," I said. "One thing I've got to say for Aragon City—it caters to every taste, including some I don't have."

"Milo," she said, all seriousness again, "who did it?"

"Three of Aragon City's Finest," I said. "Detectives Grant and Fleming and Captain Sam Logan. Each of them, in his own right, a fine man with a shillelagh."

"I know things are pretty bad here," she said. "I couldn't work for the Committee without knowing it. Or for Mr. Willis either. But do you mean they just picked you up and started beating you? Why—it's illegal!"

I grinned. That was the attitude that most people had when they heard about police third degrees.

"They made it partly legal," I said. "There was a girl murdered here in this apartment that day."

She turned pale. "Murdered?" she said. "Who?"

"Not anyone you'd know," I said. "She was what Mr. Willis would call a lady of the evening. She made her living the hard way. But she was a human being, who probably once had dreams of meeting a Prince Charming and settling down in a bungalow. But the Prince Charming turned out to be a dozen guys named Joe with fat wallets, and she settled down on a Simmons mattress. But somebody was afraid she'd talk to me, so she was killed. Then they pretended to believe I did it, and that was the excuse."

There was horror in her eyes. "What are you going to do about it, Milo?"

"Nothing directly," I said. "Or at least, not much. There's only one way to work on a case like this. That's to keep everyone off balance and they turn themselves up. That's what happened this time. Now, there's a small chance I can combine business and pleasure."

"I don't understand," she said.

I lit a cigarette and leaned back. "It's like this, Betty," I said. "I was hired by your Committee and asked to find a Mr. X. Mr. X is suspected of being some otherwise respectable citizen who is getting rich by providing protection for prostitution, the drug traffic, and gambling. But he's only the organizer of the protection. The people who really provide it, and collect part of the money he gets, are on the police force, maybe in the D.A.'s office, maybe on the City Council. Some of them have to be pretty high on the police force. But Mr. X doesn't have contact with all of his co-workers in graft. If he did, he wouldn't be Mr. X and still respectable. In fact, if he's smart, he'll be known to as few as possible. My guess is that Jan Lomer and Johnny Doll know Mr. X—they'd have to in order to be sure he's someone who can deliver. But on the other side of the fence, I'd guess that only one person knows Mr. X—the one man who picks up and delivers the payoff and who also sees that Mr. X's orders are carried out. You follow me so far?"

"Yes," she said.

"Okay," I said. "Now I arrive in town to smoke out Mr. X. The Committee think they're being very secretive about this, but it's about as big a secret as a pregnant girl in a girls' dormitory. If I start asking a lot of questions, either everybody clams up or they send me off on wild chases. But if I don't do much of anything, they get worried. They're all set to counterpunch, and I don't throw any punches. They have to find out why, and they start exposing themselves. The first ones are small fry. Like when I arrived, they tried a small frame. Two errand boys, Detectives Grant and Fleming, arrived to nail the frame in place. It didn't work, so on the next attempt, a bigger rat had to come out of the hole. And that's the way it works."

"I understand all that," she said slowly, "but what has that got to do with the police beating you?"

"The first time out, I drew Grant and Fleming," I said. "They fell on their faces, so the next time they took me to a Captain Logan. That means something just by itself. Get it?"

"All it would mean to me is that the whole police force is crooked."

I shook my head. "Don't you believe it," I said. "In any city, probably no more than five or ten percent of a police force is crooked. They give the black eye to the rest. But even with the crooked cops, a captain doesn't often take part in third degrees. So right away, it would seem to point to Logan as being an important cog in the Aragon City fix."

"I see that," she said.

"But a couple of other things cinched it," I said. "When they first took me in to see Logan, he was on the phone. He was apparently talking to the Chief of Police. And *he* was telling the Chief how things had to be. What does that tell you?"

She frowned in concentration. "Since the chief outranks a captain, it must mean that they're involved in something else in which the captain outranks the chief."

"Right," I said. "To me, it means the Chief is getting his

share of the payoff, and he's getting it from Captain Logan. But there was something else. Later, Logan got another phone call. Someone raised hell with him for working on me, and he got orders to turn me loose. He talked pretty small this time and obeyed the orders. Now, when a police captain tells his chief to go to hell, when he talks small it must be somebody pretty important. Somebody obviously bigger than anyone in the police department. So I think it means one thing. Captain Logan is the one man who knows Mr. X, and it was Mr. X who phoned him."

She looked at me and thought it over. "What are you going to do about it?" she asked.

"If I'm right," I said, "that makes Captain Logan necessary to Mr. X. Suppose Logan can't run his usual errands, for some reason or other. Business still has to go on as usual. So Mr. X will either have to run around collecting money and paying it out himself, or he'll have to find another boy. Either way, he has to come out of his hole a little."

"Is that what you mean by keeping them off balance?" she asked.

I nodded.

"But how are you going to get Captain Logan out of circulation?"

"I'll work it out," I said. "I think he needs a vacation anyway. Captain Logan has been working too hard—especially yesterday. Want to do me another favor?"

"I'll wash the dishes," she said with a smile.

"Not that," I said. "Just leave them. I'll wash them later."

"Let's do them together," she said.

And so we did. It was a domestic touch that I found myself enjoying. It's funny how something that's always been drudgery can suddenly become fun.

"Now, what was the favor?" she asked as she put away the last cup.

"You have to go to work," I said, "and I want to drop by and see the old lady, Miss Saxon. You can drive me there on your way to the office."

"Sure," she said, "but what's wrong with your car?"

I didn't like lying to her, but the less she knew about what I was doing, the safer she'd be.

"Lost, strayed, or stolen," I said. "It was real drunk out last night. Either I forgot and left my car somewhere, or it was stolen. I'll report it later."

"But I thought I saw it downstairs when I came in," she said.

I shook my head. "Must've been another one like it," I said. "That's the trouble with California—Cadillacs are so common."

She laughed and we went out. She was driving an MG, and I felt real silly folding my long legs into it. But once I got used to sitting so close to the ground, I rather liked it. She had the top down and the wind blew her red hair around her face, making as pretty a picture as you could want to see.

"Rain check?" I said to her as we drove along.

"What?" she asked. She sounded puzzled.

"Rain check," I repeated. "I was rained out last night. And the night before. I want another chance. On the date."

She laughed. "Of course, Milo. I told you I understood."

"Tonight?" I asked.

She nodded.

"No stand-up," I promised. "Cross my heart and hope to be called a cop, if I do. Neither iron bars nor wooden clubs shall keep me from my destined date."

"I accept the promise," she said. "But—but Milo—" She hesitated and seemed embarrassed.

"Yes?" I prompted.

"Be careful—will you?"

I used to think it would be horrible to have somebody worrying over me and warning me to be careful every time I went out, but I kind of liked it when she said it.

"Of course," I said. "I don't think there will be any more rough stuff now. We'll probably all conduct ourselves like bloody little gentlemen." I didn't believe it, but I made it sound as if I did.

"Same time?" she asked, after rewarding me with a little-girl smile.

"Seven-thirty," I said. "Just in case I don't have my car back by then, why don't you meet me at the apartment? Then, if I don't have my car, we can go in yours and I can feel like a kept man."

She laughed and we drove on in a kind of intimate silence that I found restful. I almost felt like a new man. My headache was still there, but it wasn't bothering me too much. I felt a little bit like a guy out for a ride with his girl instead of a guy performing on a tightrope that was liable to snap around his neck any minute.

She drove me to the old-fashioned mansion and left me there. I went up and punched the doorbell.

The same doddering old butler let me in and escorted me to the reception room. After a bit, Miss Saxon came in. Her eyes were bright, as if she enjoyed her new interest in life.

"You look younger and more beautiful every time I see you," I said, grinning, as she came in.

She liked it even though she knew it was all in fun. "Young man," she said sternly, "it's fifty years too late for that kind of talk with me. It would go better with that pretty little thing who works for the Committee."

"I've just been giving her an earful of it," I said. "But I had a little left over, and I thought I might as well spill it around."

"So," she said sharply. But I could see by the twinkle in her eyes that she didn't mean it. "Is that the way you spend your time working for the Committee?"

"Not entirely," I admitted. "I've been up to a few other things, but none of them as interesting."

"And why did you come to see an old lady?"

"Because I like the old lady," I said. "Besides, I wanted to whisper something in your shell-like ear which you can pass along to the Committee when it meets today."

"So," she said. The old girl was really enjoying herself. "You won't make any reports to the Committee, but you want to use me to plant information so you can watch the reactions. Is that it?"

"Partly," I said. "If it gets a reaction at all, it'll be a better one if it comes as something I apparently dropped while talking to you. I've discovered the man who is undoubtedly the go-between for the man we want and the ones who do the dirty work."

"Who?" she asked.

"Captain Logan." I thought about it and added, "But don't tell them his name."

"Sam Logan," she snorted. "I knew him when he used to steal apples from our backyard."

"Well, he's stealing more than apples now," I said. "I'm going to do something—never mind what—that will keep him out of circulation for a few days. Then the man at the top will have to make some new arrangements. Maybe in making them, his foot will slip a little."

"And why do you want the Committee to know this?"

"I hope I'm going to make it look as if I didn't have anything to do with it. Then only the Committee will know definitely that I did."

She nodded. "You know," she said, "I've been thinking about what you said when you were here before. About someone being on the Committee in order to know what we're doing. I know everyone on that Committee, and if one of them is up to something funny, I ought to be able to see it."

She was enjoying the idea of herself in the role of a detective so much that I hated to spoil her fun.

"No playing detective," I said. "There's a lot at stake in this, and there is going to be some rough playing before it's over. I wouldn't want you getting hurt."

"Nonsense," she said. "I can take care of myself."

"I'm sure," I said, grinning, "that in the ordinary sense that's even an understatement. But there's nothing ordinary about the people concerned. Even the top man, who is probably considered a respectable man by most people, is apt to be a killer if he's about to be exposed."

"Don't be melodramatic," the old lady said. I almost expected her to add that the people she knew couldn't be killers, but she fooled me.

"Okay," I said. "Don't say I didn't warn you."

I said good-bye and left. Down the street, I stopped in at the corner drugstore and called the D.A.'s office. The girl put him on as soon as she heard my name.

"March," he said when he came on, "your friend will be on duty at the Seventh Precinct—that's where they first took you yesterday—until six o'clock tonight. You understand, of course, that that's his own precinct and he doesn't have to be there every minute."

"I understand," I said. "But he'll have to be there to check out for the day?"

"Yes." He hesitated. "What are you up to, March?"

"Me?" I asked. "I got a hobby, that's all. I collect the schedules of important people. It's much more exciting than autographs."

"Okay," he said wearily. "Just be careful. I don't want to have to visit you at San Quentin."

"I don't like visitors anyway," I said. "What are the limits of the Seventh Precinct?"

"El Jardin Avenue on the north. On the south—"

"That's all I need," I interrupted. "Keep a habeas corpus burning in the window for me. I'll be home late."

I went out and went to a movie.

SEVEN

I saw four feature films and three newsreels. Then I went into a crummy little side-street bar and nibbled on some brandy until it was time to go. Then I walked across town. It was a long walk and my muscles were still pretty sore, but I didn't want to take the chance of using a cab. And there were no buses that would take me there.

The Cadillac was still parked on the side street. I had made certain that it was a no-limit parking zone, so it hadn't caught the eye of any traffic cops. I got in and drove back to the main part of town. I found a side street running off Ferrala Street, just two blocks from the precinct, which enabled me to watch the front of the station house. It was a dead end, so there wasn't much traffic on it. I parked, with the nose of the car pointed toward Ferrala, and waited. I left the motor running so I wouldn't have to warm the engine up.

It was about five after six when I saw him come out of the front of the station house. There was no mistaking that lumbering walk. He was alone.

He turned and walked in the opposite direction, along Ferrala Street. I pulled out and followed him, hugging the right side of the street and letting the Cadillac crawl. Traffic was light.

I was going to have to do it the hard way, unless I got one good break. I got it.

He turned left at the first intersection. He stopped on the curb and looked both ways. I was still crawling, maybe two hundred feet from him. There was one other car coming from the other direction, but the driver was already signaling a stop. There was no mistaking the blue police uniform, and California law says that pedestrians have the right of way at intersections. Drivers who normally ignore it are pretty sure to remember when the pedestrian is also a cop.

He stepped off the curb and started across the street with the air of a man who owned it.

For once I was glad the Committee had given me a Cadillac instead of a jalopy. I'd heard somewhere that the Cadillac would go from zero to sixty miles an hour in something like sixty feet. It must have been true. I jammed the accelerator to the floor. The back of the seat rammed me between the shoulders. The speedometer arm spun.

He heard the sudden roar of the motor, all right. He looked up. Then he tried to get out of the way. He was even pretty fast considering how many years he'd been polishing the seat of a chair with the gravy dripping over his badge. But when it came to pickup, he wasn't in the same class with the Cadillac.

I remembered how he'd looked when he was handling that nightstick with the towel wrapped around it. He didn't look the same now. His flabby mouth was open as if he couldn't get enough air. His red face was frozen in a twisted grimace. The fat on him quivered and heaved as he tried to leap away.

He never made it.

The left front fender caught him right where his swivel chair usually caressed him. There was a good meaty crunch as it hit, and I could feel it jar all the way up through the frame of the car. At the same time he jerked up off the street, like he was dangling from invisible strings, and flopped through the air. I caught a flash of him trying to dig his way through the pavement, then I was past the intersection.

There was a brief glimpse of the slack-jawed driver in the other car. I hit the next intersection and turned without lifting my foot from the accelerator. The tires screamed, sounding as if they might have been Logan.

I made three more turns like that, then straightened out toward the north. I slowed the car down to the legal thirty-five miles an hour.

I felt good. Maybe it was my imagination, but it seemed that my head didn't hurt so badly.

I drove across El Jardin Street, found a side street, and parked the Cadillac. I left the motor running, wiped off the steering wheel with my handkerchief, and got out. The left front fender was badly crumpled, but it looked good. I never could stand those perfect streamlined jobs.

A block away there was a bus that ran down Wilson Boulevard. I climbed on the first one that came along. It was pretty crowded and nobody paid any attention to me as I pushed through to stand by the exit door. I got off not far from the Cassandra Club.

I walked up and down the side streets for maybe ten or fifteen minutes. There were plenty of small bars around there. I looked in all of them, but finally I found one that looked just right. It was only a block from the Cassandra Club. It was small—and empty. There was a sign that said this was the

Golden Shamrock. I could see the bartender sitting back of the bar reading a magazine. The place appeared even emptier than it was. I went in.

The bartender looked as if he didn't believe it when I came in. He put aside the magazine like he thought it wasn't worth it and came over.

"Brandy," I said. "The best you've got in the house. A little water.'

He nodded and brought a bottle and two glasses. He filled one of the glasses from the tap beneath the bar. I drank the first one fast and poured myself another drink.

"How's business?" I asked.

"What business?" he asked sourly.

"Like that, huh?" I said.

"Like that." He looked at me and added, "You're the first guy in all afternoon."

That was part of what I was looking for.

"What's the matter?" I asked. "Everybody in this town dry?"

"You from out of town?" he asked.

I nodded. "Denver."

"Yeah." He looked politely interested. "I used to work in Fort Logan. Know it?"

"Nice little town," I said.

"Wish to hell I was back there," he said. "If this keeps up, I will be."

"What's the trouble?" I asked as if I didn't care. "The big club up the street?"

"That's part of it," he said. He didn't look as if he were going to say any more on his own.

"Juice?" I asked.

He looked at me with more interest. "Juice," he said. "This is strictly a copper's town. There ain't a cop in town that doesn't have his hand out. They got such long fingers they could goose the eagle on a quarter without standing on tiptoe."

"I'd heard that," I said. "You don't play, huh?"

"You're damn right I don't," he said angrily. "I've been through that rat race before. You start paying a cop and he keeps wanting more. Then he begins to get the idea of coming around for free drinks and cuffed meals. Then he sends his friends. So your customers stop coming because they don't like to drink with a bunch of cops around. ... I tell them all to drop dead."

"And?" I prodded.

He indicated the empty bar with a sweep of his hand. "You're looking at it. They come and stand around in uniform. They drag me down to the station house three times, claiming I've been serving fairies. Once they backed up the wagons and took all the customers down to the lineup. I'm going broke, but there ain't going to be a single goddam cop make a nickel off me."

"I know how it is," I said sympathetically. "I'm temporarily working out of the D.A.'s office."

He pulled a curtain over his face. "I didn't say nothing," he said flatly.

"I didn't hear anything," I said.

We looked at each other and we both grinned. He poured himself a drink from my bottle.

"What do you want?" he asked. "You want something. I can smell it."

"If you can hold out a little," I said, "maybe you'll be in business. There's going to be a new look in Aragon City. You ever see a badge after it's been dry-cleaned? It gets smaller."

"What do you want?" he asked. He wasn't antagonistic—just curious.

I reached into my pocket and pulled out my money. I took out a hundred-dollar bill and put it on the bar. I stuck the edge of it under the bottle.

"Pretty, ain't it?" I said.

"What do you want?" he repeated patiently.

"It's like this," I said. "I've been sitting up with a sick cop. I think he's just taken a turn for the worse. I wouldn't want his friends to get the wrong idea. I've been trying to think where it was I spent the afternoon drinking. I think this was the place. I knew it was something with a shamrock in the name."

He looked at me steadily. "What about the sick cop?" he asked.

I grinned. "He was so busy getting sick, he wasn't paying any attention to visitors. Rude. But then cops are like that."

"How come you were down this way?" he asked.

"Looking for my car that was stolen last night," I said. "But I guess I might as well report it now."

He reached out and took the hundred-dollar bill.

"You know," he said without changing his expression, "this is the first time I ever saw a guy drink brandy all afternoon and carry it so well."

"It's experience," I said. I slid down off the stool. I started for the door. "Thanks," I said.

"Any time, pal," he called after me. "There's only one thing I like better than C-notes. That's sick cops."

I went out and walked to Wilson Boulevard. My guess was that he'd stand by the story, even more than a hundred dollars' worth. But I also had a notion it wouldn't even be needed. It was just that I wanted a little insurance.

I got a cab on Wilson Boulevard and had him drive me to the Seventh Precinct. Everything was quiet on the street. I could sense a little excitement inside the station house, but that was all. The desk sergeant wasn't the same one who'd greeted me the day before. He looked bored when I told him I wanted to report a stolen car.

"Where and when?" he asked.

"Last night. In front of the Cassandra Club on Wilson."

"Why'd you take so long to report it?" he asked.

I produced a sheepish grin. "Well, to tell the truth," I said, "I had a little too much under my belt last night. This morning I wasn't sure if maybe I just left it. So I went down and looked around. By that time I needed a little of the hair, and I guess it took a while to get up a head of steam so I could make it back here."

He grinned sympathetically and asked me for the particulars. I told him the make and model and the license number. Then, for identification, I showed him the card from the D.A.'s office. His grin grew broader.

"The D.A. ought to be careful," he said, "sending his boys out without police protection. There ought to be a law against it."

"I know," I deadpanned. "We lose more investigators that way."

I walked out and went home. It was almost time for my date. I just had time for a quick shower and a change of clothes. And a short brandy. Then the buzzer sounded.

I opened the door and it was Betty Carr. Now she was wearing a green and rust outfit that brought out all the fire in her hair. It didn't do any harm to her figure either. She looked kind of excited.

"Milo, did you do it?" she asked the minute she was inside.

"Do what?" I asked innocently.

"Hit Captain Logan."

"Logan," I said. I shook my head seriously. "Not exactly. You see, it was like this. Captain Logan had a nightstick wrapped up in a towel, and it's true that I hit that a number of times with my head, but that's all."

"Milo, you idiot," she said, "that's not what I mean. Somebody ran Captain Logan down with a car this evening and hurt him."

"No!" I said, putting a lot of feeling in it.

It wasn't exactly Academy stuff, but it was pretty good acting. But I could see she wasn't completely convinced.

"What happened?" I asked.

So she told me how some terrible character had run over Captain Logan while he was crossing the street and then had sped away. There had been one witness, and his description made the runaway driver sound like an ugly Frankenstein monster. I resisted the impulse to run and look in the mirror.

"You left out the most important thing," I said. "How badly was the poor captain hurt?"

"Pretty badly," she said seriously. "Both of his legs were broken. One shoulder dislocated. And he has a lot of cuts and bruises, and he's suffering from shock."

"Tch, tch," I said. "I must remember to send him flowers."

"You did do it!" she exclaimed. "You said you were going to put him out of circulation. Why did you do such a foolish thing, Milo—just for revenge?"

"Look, honey," I said, "for you, for the record, and for anybody else who asks, I didn't do it. My car was stolen last night. I went down looking for it today and spent most of the afternoon in a bar. I'm covered."

She still didn't know whether to believe me or not.

"Mr. Willis thinks you did it, too," she said. "He was furious."

"Why?"

"He said that kind of thing could ruin the Committee. He was all for calling you before the Committee at once, but Miss Saxon wouldn't let him."

"I gather," I said, "that Miss Saxon told the Committee my theories concerning Captain Logan?"

"Yes."

"Good," I said. "But Mr. Willis should watch his blood pressure. It's liable to boil over on him."

The telephone rang. I walked over and picked up the receiver. It was the District Attorney.

"Did you do it?" he asked.

"Do what?" I asked again. I was beginning to enjoy myself.

"Don't be an idiot," he snapped. "Did you put Logan in the hospital?"

"Why, whatever made you think that?" I asked.

"I just learned about your stolen car report," he said. "Filed an hour after the accident. This is phony as hell, March. I'll lay fifty to five that when they find your car there'll be a dent in it and the lab will find some blue uniform threads."

"I never gamble," I said piously. "It's illegal."

He swore. "I don't even care if you answer that question," he added, "but I do want you to answer this one. Can they pin it on you?"

"No," I said. "At least, I'm pretty certain they can't. I don't even think they'll try very hard. Now, I want you to do something else for me."

"What?"

"Put a bug on his phone," I said. "It might make interesting noises."

"The things you ask me to do," he snapped. "You know damn well it's illegal to tap telephones. And there could be a hell of a stink if I tap the hospital's lines and it's found out."

"I know," I said.

There was a long silence.

"As a matter of fact," he said finally, "I've already done it. Ten minutes after he was admitted."

I was surprised. "My boy," I said, "if you ever want to run for president, you got my vote right in your pocket."

"You fall down on this, March," he warned, "and you're going to be in a darker place than that. And the only place I'll ever be able to run for office is in Liberia. Good-bye."

He hung up.

"Who was that?" Betty asked.

"A friend of mine," I said. I wasn't being evasive. I meant it more than anything I'd said in a long time. "You ready to go find that dinner we missed a couple of days ago?"

She smiled. "Yes."

I walked over to take her arm. She was wearing some sort of light perfume that went right to my head. Maybe it was because of an empty stomach, but I don't think so.

I swung her gently around and into my arms. Then I kissed her. Her lips held back a little, but not too much. She wasn't selling anything, but that kiss wiped out the memory of any other kisses that were still cluttering up my reminiscences.

I held her away from me and looked at her. Her eyes were a little brighter and I could feel the little quiver in her arms where I held them.

"We could stay here," I said.

She shook her head. "No, Milo," she said softly. She pulled back out of my arms. "I'll be honest with you. I'd like to … stay with you. But if I ever do that, I've got to know that it's real. I don't want any secondhand honeymoons filling up my hope chest. Not any more, Milo."

I surprised myself by nodding. "Have you ever thought it was real?" I asked her. I surprised myself even more with that one. It was the first time I'd ever given a damn.

"Once," she said. Her voice sounded far away.

"What happened?" I asked gently.

"I don't know," she said. "Something got tarnished somewhere along the line. That's why I'm going to have to be sure the next time—if there is a next time."

"There will be," I said.

She came back from wherever she was and gave me a smile. "You're sweet, Milo," she said. "Now let's go get that dinner." We went. Back to the Cassandra Club.

EIGHT

The steak was wonderful. So was everything else—including Betty. We ate dinner slowly, talking about a lot of unimportant things. It was the kind of getting acquainted that is all fun. There was none of the challenge, the feeling of playing a game, that goes with a situation when you're strictly on the make. By the time we reached coffee and brandy, I knew all about her family and she knew the high spots of Milo March prior to Aragon City.

"And this," I concluded, "is where you came in. Now, if we can only clear the house of the popcorn munchers, we can start the feature film. Or are you bored?"

"I'm not bored, Milo," she said. "But I'm not sure that I've got the right ticket."

"You've got it," I said. "I ought to know. I sold it to you."

She laughed. It was a nice laugh, warm and intimate and full of promise.

I looked up and saw them. They were coming across the club, weaving around the tables but heading for our table. A paunchy, tired-looking man and a skinny, hungry-looking one. I slipped the gun from my holster and held it under the napkin on my lap.

"Here comes Aragon City's Finest," I said softly to Betty. "Hold on to your purse."

She looked around and her face tightened. She was frightened, but she held on.

They came to the table and pulled out the other two chairs. They sat down without saying anything.

"You'll forgive us for having eaten?" I asked. "We were afraid you weren't coming."

My tone of voice was completely lost on those two.

"Who's the dame?" Harry Fleming asked, jerking a broad thumb in the direction of Betty.

"Harry," Grant said, "how many times must I tell you that's no way to talk about a lady. She's the broad who works in the Civic *Betterment* Committee's office."

"Nice work if you can get it," Fleming said. Both of them were keeping their eyes fixed on me.

"You couldn't get it," I said.

Harry Fleming leaned forward, looking tired. "March, you're a son of a bitch," he said.

"I like you, too," I said. "Shall I save the next dance?"

"You're a son of a bitch," he repeated doggedly.

"He means," Grant explained, "that we've found your *stolen* car."

"You have!" I exclaimed. "And you two boys took the trouble to run all the way down here to tell me? That was real sweet of you. Maybe I've misjudged you boys."

"We found it," Grant continued, "on Borchard Street, just off El Jardin Street. The left front fender was pretty badly dented. Like maybe it hit somebody."

"People who steal cars," I said, "are apt to go from bad to worse. The next thing you know they're killing people and maybe even becoming cops."

"You," said Harry Fleming, his voice thick, "are the son

of a bitch who ran down Sam Logan and put him in the hospital."

"Not good old Sam!" I said. "You don't mean to tell me that he's in the hospital? I must remember to send him some flowers. Do you think he'd like pansies?"

"Cut the stalling," Grant said harshly. "We know that you got Logan. We know that you bragged that you were going to put him out of circulation, and we know you were in the car when it hit him. The only thing we're interested in is, can we prove it?"

"No," I said. I gave him my best smile.

"Captain Logan was struck at 6:05," Grant continued. "You claim that your car was stolen last night, but you didn't report it until 7:10. Why?"

"I went looking for it," I said. "That tired me out and I went into a bar and built up my strength with brandy. I was there all afternoon—until about 6:30, in fact."

"An alibi, huh?" Grant said. "Alibis have been broken."

"So have cops," I said.

"You know what I think," Fleming said. His hands were clenched tightly. "I think we ought to take you in right now. Then I think we ought to take you to a nice quiet place and *question* you. A place that ain't got a telephone."

"That would be a good idea," I said, "if you could do it."

His face got darker. "We can take you," he said.

I raised the napkin above the edge of the table, resting my hand by my plate. It was a perfectly normal gesture to everyone else in the restaurant, but I knew they could see the gun. Their eyes tightened a little and that was all.

"Can you?" I asked.

We sat like that for maybe two minutes. I could hear the breath rasping in Fleming's throat.

"Okay," Grant said finally. His voice was flat. "We just wanted to tell you about your car. You can pick it up at the precinct anytime you want to."

"Thanks," I said.

They got up from the table, moving very carefully. They pushed the chairs back. Grant had to nudge Fleming a little, but they both turned and left. I saw Grant wave to someone at the bar, but Fleming just plowed ahead like a man with something on his mind.

Then I turned to look at Betty for the first time since they had arrived. She was pale and I thought she was shaking, but she was riding it out like a trouper.

"I'm sorry, honey," I said.

"It's all right, Milo," she said. Her voice was a little thin, but it grew stronger as she went along. "What did you do that made them change their mind?"

I lifted the edge of the napkin and let her see the gun. Then I slipped it back into the holster.

"I doubt if they would have taken me anyway," I said. "Fleming would have, but I think Grant would have stopped him. They're getting a little edgy now—which is just the way I want them."

"But won't they do something?" she asked.

"Cops always do something," I answered. "Usually they make idiots of themselves."

She laughed. There was still a little nervousness in her voice, but not much.

"Silly," she said. "Seriously, Milo, aren't they dangerous?"

"Only if you leave them around loaded," I said. "But to hell with the cops. To hell with Aragon City. Let's talk about something important. You and me, for instance."

But before we could start on the important things, a waiter came over to our table. He wanted to know if I was Mr. March. I said I was. He said there was a phone call for me.

I thought about it. Nobody knew that I was at the Cassandra Club. I hadn't even known myself that I was going there until we started. But the two detectives had come to the club to see me. And now somebody was calling me. Maybe someone was publishing hourly bulletins on me. I thought, to hell with them. What could I lose by a phone call?

"I'll take it," I told the waiter.

"I'm sorry, sir," he said, "but the call did not come in over the regular number, so I can't bring the phone to your table. We have one phone booth here and that's where the call came."

"Where is it?" I asked.

"Next to the bar, sir," he said. He pointed.

It was at the near end of the bar. There were plenty of customers around. Maybe it was a trap and maybe it wasn't. I'd never know unless I found out.

"Okay," I said. I stood up and grinned at Betty. "I'll be right back, honey."

I walked across the floor toward the bar. As I got nearer, I could see the phone receiver hanging from the cord. I didn't see anyone I knew among the customers.

I stepped into the booth, without bothering to close the door, and picked up the receiver.

"Yeah?" I said.

"Milo March?" a strange man's voice asked.

"Yeah," I said. "Who's this?"

There was a hesitation. Then he hung up.

I knew then it was a trap. I let the receiver fall, but it was already too late. Something was nudging against my ribs. Something hard.

"Relax, pal," a voice said softly.

I looked around, turning my head slowly. It was Rudy Cioppa, Johnny Doll's pet. His face was as expressionless as ever, but I got the impression he was happy. He was leaning into the booth. There was a newspaper folded carelessly over his right arm and hand. It covered the gun he was pressing against me.

"I'll take the extra weight," he said. He reached over with his left hand and snaked my gun out of its holster. He dropped it in his pocket.

"That was real cute," I said. "Who was your friend?"

"A guy," he said. "He called from one of the tables."

"Cute," I repeated. "But then you're a cute kid. Have you got a bicycle?"

"What's the gag?" he asked.

"You get around," I explained. "I thought maybe you had a bicycle."

"Very funny," he said. Maybe he thought so, but his lips didn't even twitch. "Let's go."

"Where?"

"Around," he said. "Back out of there real easy-like. Then we walk out of the club together."

"Just like good old pals," I said. "Like that, huh?"

"Like that," he agreed. He backed off from the booth a little. His eyes were bright—too bright. I knew he was ready.

I came out of the booth—carefully. As I stepped out, I flashed a look through the club. Betty had just left the table, headed for the ladies' room. She didn't see me.

"I guess it's not my night," I said. "Okay."

We walked past the bar and nobody paid any attention to us. The point of the gun never left my ribs. Rudy walked close and a little behind me. We went through the door and out of the club.

A big sedan was parked in front of the club, its motor running. I recognized the guy behind the wheel. It was the guy from Johnny Doll's store. The one Rudy had called Manny.

We got into the back seat of the car. Rudy sat sidewise on the seat and shook the newspaper off his hand. The street light came through the window enough to glint from the blue barrel.

"Okay, Manny," Rudy said. The car took off with a smooth surge of power.

"Where are we going?" I asked.

"A little drive in the country."

"Well, they say the country air is healthy," I said.

"It might be," he agreed. "It's up to you."

That told me something. Not much, but a little. They at least going to talk to me before they thought about turning me into a target. *That* was something I hadn't counted on. The way I'd looked at it, Jan Lomer and Mr. X would do almost anything to keep it short of killing. There was too much heat on, with Senator Kefauver's Committee still nosing around, for them to risk having a dead investigator on their hands. But, of course, there was still the chance that Johnny Doll might take the bit in his teeth. That was what Captain Sam Logan had apparently done, and Johnny Doll seemed as impetuous.

I remembered something else.

"Rudy," I said, "was it you that Grant waved to when he left my table?"

"I know Grant," Rudy said. "A fine fellow."

"Oh, sterling," I said. So that was it. Grant had signaled for Rudy to take me. If I hadn't had my eyes so full of orange blossoms, I would have made something of that wave in time. I made a resolution never to get interested in a woman when I was on another job. *If* I was ever on another job. Or maybe I'd just stay interested in the same woman now.

"How come," I asked Rudy, more to hear the sound of my own voice than anything else, "you like cops? You'll lose your fraternity pin if you aren't careful."

"There are cops and cops," he said. Rudy was a great conversationalist.

"That's a profound statement," I admitted.

"Some cops I don't like," he said. He hesitated just long enough and then added, "You're a cop."

"That was unkind of you, Rudy," I said. "Why should you call me dirty names?"

He grunted, and the conversation, if you could call it that, sort of fell apart at the seams.

We drove north through Santa Monica and then began

winding up the hills beyond Santa Monica Canyon. It was a nice drive, but it was no place to be if you were going to have to yell for help.

After a while our headlights picked out a car parked beside the street. We swerved in behind it and cut our lights. A figure detached itself from the other car and walked back. It was Johnny Doll.

"Any trouble?" he asked, slipping into the front seat and turning to face the back.

"No trouble," Rudy Cioppa said.

"Good." He shifted his gaze to look at me. It was dark in the car and his face was a shadowy blob beneath the broad-brimmed hat. "I wanted to see you, March."

"I sort of got that general idea," I said.

"Nobody around here seems to know how to handle a punk like you except me," he said. He sounded petulant. "Jan Lomer had to have a nice, polite talk with you, and what happens? You go right on raising hell. Then those jerk cops give you the works, and what happens? You damn near kill Logan. I'm tired of telling them how to do it. I'm taking over as of now. You and me talk the same language, March."

"Is that what it is?" I asked.

"Don't be a wise guy," he snapped. "I don't waste no time with all this fancy talk. You're nosing around trying to clean up Aragon City. We don't want it cleaned up. You're playing hell with business. You're making everybody nervous."

"Try phenobarbital," I suggested.

"What for?"

"It calms down the nerves," I said. "Wonderful stuff."

"I got something better," he said. "There's a plane taking off from Los Angeles Airport for Denver in about fifty minutes. The boys can drive you there in forty minutes, maybe less. There's a ticket at the desk for you. It's all paid for."

"What about my luggage?" I asked.

"We'll pack it up and send it to you," he said.

"That's mighty nice of you," I said. I didn't feel as casual as I sounded, but I wasn't going to let them know. "But I'm afraid I'll have to turn it down."

"Why?"

"I promised my mother I'd never take money from strangers," I said. "You wouldn't want me to break my promise, would you?"

"Okay," Johnny Doll said. His voice had hardened. "You're a smart bastard with the answers. But we've got one we haven't tried on you yet. ... He's your meat, Rudy."

He slipped from the front seat and walked back toward the car ahead.

I wedged one shoulder against the side of the car and waited. I knew that this was the showdown and that I wasn't ready for it because I hadn't expected it yet. But maybe if I timed myself right I could still come out of it in one piece. I'd have to get both of them in one move, and it would have to be good.

We sat there while Johnny Doll's car pulled away, the twin red lights finally winking out around a curve somewhere ahead.

"Here?" Manny asked from the front seat.

"Why not?" said Rudy. "One place is as good as another. You don't care where it happens, do you, sucker?"

"Me?" I asked. "I got only one request to make. Couldn't we put this off long enough for me to order a Bond Street tuxedo from London? I've always wanted to go out in style."

I had slowly shifted around on the seat until I figured I was in as good a position as I'd ever be in. I'd swing my right foot for Rudy's head and then go for Manny. It looked good—in theory.

"One thing you got to say for him," Rudy said. "He's got guts. It's a pleasure to polish off a guy like this."

"Playboy," I snapped.

"Hold it a minute," Manny said. "There's a car coming. Wait until it gets by."

"Okay," Rudy said.

We all waited while the headlights drew closer behind us, throwing weird shadows inside the car.

I decided to make my play just as the car passed. Some of their attention would be on it and I'd never get a better chance. I braced myself.

The car was really traveling fast. It swept around the last gradual curve behind us and fairly leaped at us. It seemed to slacken, then its tires were skidding on the dry road.

"Manny," Rudy said sharply, "watch it."

"Got it," Manny said.

It looked like the play was being taken out of my hands. Despite its speed, the other car was stopping in about three times its own length. Whoever was in the car thought they were looking for us. I didn't have any idea who it could be, but right then I didn't mind being looked for. Whatever happened, it was bound to be an improvement.

The car stopped even with us and the big body visibly settled back down on its rear springs. The back door opened and a man got out. I couldn't see his face, but I could see he was big. He walked toward us.

"Hold it," Rudy said in a low voice. "It's Lomer."

He came up to the car and leaned against it, looking inside.

"Ah, good evening, Mr. March," he said. "I thought perhaps I'd find you here. I trust that my intrusion is not unwelcome."

"I can't say that it is," I said. "In fact, if you were prettier, I'd kiss you."

He chuckled.

"What's the idea, Lomer?" Rudy Cioppa asked. He tried to sound tough and respectful at the same time. "Johnny ain't going to like this."

"Probably not," Jan Lomer said. "But he'll put up with it, even as will you, my trigger-happy friend. I'm an old man, Rudy, but I'm still able to handle three or four like you. Do you care to dispute the matter with me?"

When you're around it enough, fear becomes something you can smell. Only a few minutes before I could smell my own, but now it was Rudy's. I knew that Rudy Cioppa was a man who seldom knew fear, but he was afraid of Jan Lomer. He had a gun right in his hand and the old man had no gun in sight, but Rudy was still afraid.

"It's your play," he said sullenly. "But Johnny ain't going to like it."

"I will tell Johnny myself," Jan Lomer said, "but if you see him first, you might tell him that if he's not careful he's going to be out of business. And you, too. ... Mr. March?"

"Yes, Mr. Lomer," I said, feeling like half of a new Gallagher and Shean vaudeville team.*

"Would you care to come into my car?"

"I wouldn't mind," I said. He chuckled again as I was getting out. My legs were still a little weak, but I managed to make it without stumbling. When I was on the road, I turned back for a minute.

"It was nice knowing you, Rudy," I said. "Would you mind giving me my gun? We might meet again, and I'd hate to think that you still owed me anything."

He hesitated, looking at Jan Lomer. But then he took the gun from his pocket and handed it to me.

"I owe you something, all right," he said. His voice was a little hoarse.

"On the contrary, Rudy," I said. "I insist that the next time we have a party, it has to be my treat."

I climbed into the back seat of the other car and Jan Lomer got in after me. The driver looked like the man who had served the eggs the day I had lunch with Lomer, but it was too dark to be sure. The car started forward.

"I owe you an apology, Mr. March," he said. "Not only for this blunder of Johnny Doll's, but for the fact that you were beaten by certain officers the other day. It is one of the penalties, sir, which I must suffer because of being forced to do business with men who are the scum of the earth. No brains, Mr. March."

"Your arrival was the only apology I needed," I said. "But how did you know where to find us?"

---

* The 1920s vaudeville duo were famous for their theme song, with its tagline "Absolutely, Mister Gallagher?" "Positively, Mister Shean!"

"The man who helped Rudy Cioppa trap you in a phone booth has perhaps an ounce more of brains than the others. He began to realize that Johnny Doll might be operating on his own. So he phoned me. He knew which road you were taking."

"A wonderful invention, the telephone," I said.

"You'll forgive me, sir, for not arriving sooner," he said. "I'm aware that those situations can be trying." That was an understatement if I'd ever heard one.

"It's okay," I said. "Although it's true if you had arrived much later, I would have been deeply wounded."

His laughter filled the car. "I like you, Mr. March," he said. "Do you mind if we go to my house for a few minutes? I have a few things I'd like to discuss with you."

"Okay," I said.

We drove the rest of the way in silence. When we arrived at the house, we went into that same study—the one with the fine books, the rare pieces of artwork. I took the same chair I'd sat in before and lit a cigarette. Jan Lomer once more sat back of the desk.

"Mr. March," he said, "I intend to be entirely frank with you. As you know, I am part of a national syndicate. The Combine, some call us. This is not, as many have guessed, an organized corporation of crime. For the most part, the business here on the West Coast belongs to Johnny Doll and myself. But the members of the Syndicate share mutual investments, give a certain amount of aid and assistance to each other, and are fully aware that our destinies are held in common."

"I knew it was about like that," I said.

"There was a time, sir, not so long ago, when businesses such as this were conducted with more violence than efficiency. But we became aware that the resulting publicity was bad. That is why I am keeping Johnny Doll from doing as he wishes. Were you to be murdered, Mr. March, it might cause more attention to be focused on us when we can ill afford it. I have been discussing you with members of the Syndicate in the East and the Midwest. We do not want you killed, Mr. March."

"I'm touched," I said.

"On the other hand, sir, your present activities are also bad for us. You're costing us money. Therefore, we've decided to do business with you."

"Meaning what?" I asked.

He leaned forward. "Mr. March, you told me that you were interested in only one thing in Aragon City—getting the man who sells us protection. Is that correct?"

"It is," I said.

"Then we are prepared to assist you. We will name this man for you—although I imagine you already have a good idea who he is. We will also furnish any amount of evidence necessary for your case, so long as it does not involve any essential member of our organization. In return, you will give me your word that once you have this information, you will report it and leave Aragon City."

I thought it over. "You know," I said, "I could promise you that, but turn in more."

"Not easily, sir," he said. "You could not get more information without considerable more work than you're doing. And if you insisted on staying here, I would have no choice but to let the ideas of Johnny Doll prevail."

"Okay," I said. "Who's the man?"

"Your word, sir?"

There was something about this I didn't like. I wasn't sure what it was, but I wanted to protect myself in the clinches.

"Let's put it this way," I said. "If you turn a man over to me and I'm satisfied that he's *the* man, then I'll agree."

He looked at me for a minute. "The man," he said, "is Captain Sam Logan, of the Aragon City Police."

"Offhand," I said carefully, "it sounds to me like you're putting a man's shoes on a boy."

"I give you my word, sir," he said, "that Logan is the man we've been paying."

"That I believe. Logan is big, all right, but I don't think he's as big as you're selling him. Logan's too easy to see."

He studied me. "Mr. March," he said, "what do you want? The mayor of Aragon City?"

"Could I get him if I'd settle for that?" I asked. I was curious.

"Yes," he said.

I rolled that one over in my mind. The pressure must be really on if they were willing to make that sort of deal.

"I'm sure," I said, "that the mayor is in on this somewhere along the line. Maybe he's the top, maybe he isn't. If he is, the question is why are you willing to toss him into the pot?"

"This sort of thing is bad for business, sir," he said. "In order to see the matter peaceably terminated, we're willing to make a sacrifice or two. I might add, sir, that it is completely unimportant to us who is in political power in Aragon City. We can always find someone with whom we can do business. You will recall, Mr. March, that I mentioned that this is a corrupt society."

"I remember," I said. I didn't like any part of this. I didn't doubt that there was pressure coming from the Syndicate, but I had a feeling there was some more pressure being put on Lomer to help set up a sacrificial lamb. I had an idea that the small fry was getting nervous and that somebody wanted the matter to look closed.

"Tell me something else," I said. "If I agreed to settle for Captain Sam Logan and if Logan isn't really the top man, there'd be danger of him talking. I'm convinced that Logan does know the top man and is the only one who does know. At least on the other side of the fence. He might not like to be led to the slaughter. He might talk."

"We'd take care of that," Lomer said. I knew what he meant.

"You mean a dead local cop wouldn't smell as bad as an imported investigator?"

"My boy," he said, "you underestimate us. Look at it this way—take a crooked police captain who is exposed. He's very apt to commit suicide. There's a very high suicide rate among policemen, you know."

"Yeah—I've always been in favor of it," I said.

He shook with laughter. With this guy I had a higher Hooper rating than Bob Hope.

"Let me sum it up," I went on. "The way things are stacked, I'd better finish this job up quick. And I have a choice between Captain Logan and the mayor of Aragon City. Is that it?"

"Succinctly put, sir," he said. "I trust that you appreciate that I don't believe in pinching a man too tightly. That's why you have a choice of victims."

"Some choice," I said. "I have a couple of other scores to settle. Two detectives by the names of Grant and Fleming."

"Do as you like, sir. When it comes to policemen of such low rank, we buy them wholesale." This time he laughed at his own joke.

"Well," I said, standing up, "I'd like to think about it overnight. All right?"

"Perfectly, sir. Will you join me in a brandy before you go?"

"No, thanks," I said, surprising even myself. "I was with a young lady when Rudy took me in tow. She may be worried."

"My man is waiting outside in the car," Jan Lomer said. "He will take you anywhere you want to go."

"Thanks," I said. "I'll call you tomorrow. Probably late in the afternoon."

"I shall look forward to it," he said. "I like you, Mr. March. I trust we shall be able to conclude this matter upon a most amicable basis."

"Me too," I said. I went out of the house and climbed into his limousine. I told the driver to take me to the Cassandra Club.

I guessed that Betty was probably gone by this time, and she was. I went back out and had Lomer's man drive me home. I thought of picking up my own car, but decided to wait until the following morning.

I went upstairs and made myself comfortable, with a bottle of brandy beside me. I would have liked to call Betty and explain things to her, but realized that the only number I had for her was the one at the Committee's offices. So I sipped my brandy and thought about my visit with Jan Lomer.

About thirty minutes later the phone rang. I picked up the receiver and said hello.

"Milo, are you all right?" It was Betty and she sounded frightened.

"Sure, honey," I said. "I was just sitting here thinking what a poor date-risk I am. The first time I don't show up at all, and the second time I walk out on you in the middle of the date. Nice guy, March!"

"Oh, that!" she said. "What happened?"

"You're a real sweetheart," I said and meant it. "What makes you sure that I'm not just a heel who walked out on you?"

"You wouldn't do it," she said firmly. "When you didn't come back, I knew something had happened. Finally I came home, and I've been calling your number every half hour or so. Thank God you finally answered."

"Would it really have made much difference?" I asked her. I felt like a high school boy talking to his girl, and I liked it.

"Yes," she said. Her voice was low.

"I suppose you paid the check at the club, too?" I asked.

"Of course."

"Well, I owe you that, too," I said. "As for the rest I owe you, I'll have to work at paying it off for a long time."

"That might be nice," she said. "But you haven't told me what happened."

"The phone call was a booby trap," I said, "and I walked right into it. I was taken for a ride in the best tradition."

"What happened?"

"Nothing, but a lot of talk, mostly with people who will never win any prizes as conversationalists. But I had one interesting offer. I was offered the head of Aragon City protection with full proof."

"Who?" she asked breathlessly.

"In fact, I was given a choice," I said. "I can have either Captain Logan or the mayor of Aragon City. On a platter."

She was silent for a minute. "Does that mean you don't think it's on the level?" she asked finally.

"About as level as the Tower of Pisa," I said. "But it was a nice offer."

"What are you going to do about it, Milo?"

"Right now, I'm thinking about it," I said. "Not very seriously, but I'm sort of looking it over. I'm afraid it's not a very good fit, though. If I don't take it, I've got to move pretty fast. I'm going to think about that, too."

"Want me to come over and help you think?" she asked hesitatingly.

"Honey," I said fervently, "I'd like nothing better. But if you come over, I'm only going to do one kind of thinking. Remember when you came to pick me up this evening? I guess I'd better see you tomorrow."

"All right," she said quietly. "Good night, Milo."

"Good night, honey," I said.

I hung up the receiver and went back to my brandy and thinking. That was the hell of it with having to work.

When I'd thought the bottle down to the halfway mark, I knocked off and went to bed.

NINE

The next morning I went over to the precinct and picked up the Cadillac. Word must have gotten around the station house that I was the boy who'd bent their captain's bars, for I was greeted with all the enthusiasm of a dormitory matron welcoming a white slaver. They made me wait as long as possible and then put me through a process of identification which was as involved as they could think up on the spur of the moment. Finally, a sergeant took me out to the car. The fender was still rumpled and it was out of gas, but otherwise it was all right. I made a big show of checking over everything, even to looking suspiciously through everything in the dash compartment.

"What's the matter?" the sergeant asked.

"Nothing's missing," I said in tones of exaggerated surprise. "This must be an honest precinct."

He told me what I could do to myself and marched back into the station house. The back of his neck was a mottled red. It brightened up my whole day.

I got a can of gas from a nearby station and trudged back to the precinct garage. Then I drove downtown and went to the D.A.'s office.

When I asked for Yale, the receptionist told me he was tied up but wanted me to wait. She handed me a large manila envelope.

"Mr. Yale said to give this to you, Mr. March," she said. "He said that this was all they got up to this morning."

I thanked her and went over to a comfortable chair. I opened the envelope and took out some typed sheets of paper. They were transcripts of phone conversations. They bore the date of the day before. I started reading.

Conversation between Captain Logan and unidentified man
Time: 8:15

MAN: Sam don't mention any names.

LOGAN: What do you think I am, a fool?

MAN: Yes.

LOGAN: What the hell do you mean?

MAN: I mean that you've acted like an idiot from the start of this. If you hadn't tried to frame March and if you hadn't beaten him up, you probably wouldn't have had this accident. March wouldn't have even known about you if you'd been content to take orders. The next time you step out of line, you're through.

LOGAN: Okay, okay. (Pause.) It was March, then? He was the one who run me down?

MAN: It must have been. He made the statement that he was going to put you out of circulation.

LOGAN: I'll get the bastard if—

MAN: You'll do nothing of the kind. We're in enough trouble as it is. Who's going to handle protection and pick up collections with you in the hospital?

LOGAN: Grant and Fleming can handle the protection, all right. Why can't you collect the money?

MAN: That's what March wants, you idiot. The whole reason for getting you out of the way was an attempt to make me pick up the collections.

LOGAN: I never thought of that. (Pause.) Look, maybe we could have them bring the collections here to me.

MAN: Might as well arrange for the payoff to be made on the steps of City Hall. Never mind, I'll think of something. And on anything else I'll call Grant and Fleming direct.

LOGAN: Okay.

MAN: If anyone from the Syndicate calls you about a collection, stall them until I think of something.

LOGAN: Want me to phone you if I hear from them?

MAN: How many times have I told you never to phone me through a switchboard? I'll phone you tomorrow.

LOGAN: What are you going to do about March?

MAN: He won't cause much more trouble. He wouldn't have caused as much as he did if it hadn't been for you and Doll. We're going to let March be successful.

LOGAN: What?

MAN: I've been talking to Lomer about it. We're going to turn someone over to March. Maybe His Honor. He's been getting a pretty share for doing nothing anyway. Or maybe someone else.

LOGAN: Say, that's pretty smart. Who thought of that?

MAN: Not you, certainly. But if you leave things alone, we'll have March sewed up before long.

LOGAN: We'd better. (Pause.) Say, I just thought of something else.

MAN: What?

LOGAN: We'd better not drop official interest in him too quick. He'll know something's up if we don't even show any interest in him after this.

MAN: Maybe you have something at that. Okay, let your boys question him. But no rough stuff. Remember that.

LOGAN: Sure. I'll just have the boys go over to his place this evening and ask him a few polite questions.

MAN: All right. Tell them they can find March at the Cassandra Club. But no pulling him in for questioning.

LOGAN: Sure. They'll play it smart.

MAN: They better. I'll phone you tomorrow, Sam.

That was all on that one. There was a separate page on which there was typed a notation that Captain Logan had called the hospital superintendent at 8:25 and said he was going to be using his phone a lot on police business and he wanted to be sure that none of the switchboard operators listened in on his calls. Then there was one more incoming call.

Conversation between Captain Logan and Grant
Time: 8:30

GRANT: Hi, Sam. This is Grant. How you feeling?

LOGAN: Lousy. How do you expect me to feel? What did you find out?

GRANT: Nothing that means anything. There was only one witness. His description of the driver could fit anybody from King Kong to Jack the Ripper. He never thought of trying to see the license plate. But for my money it was March.

LOGAN: I can figure that myself. What I want is proof, not your guesses.

GRANT: He's a cute one, that March. You know what he did?

LOGAN: I know what I wish he'd do.

GRANT: He was in here right after seven to claim his car was stolen. Says it was lifted last night.

LOGAN: Why didn't he report it earlier, then?

GRANT: He had a fancy story. I'll bet it would stick, too. I'll even bet he's got himself a good alibi.

LOGAN: I never saw an alibi that couldn't be broken.

GRANT: You want me and Harry to go to work on him?

LOGAN: No. We've got orders to treat him like a goddam little gentleman. Question him, but don't do any more than that.

GRANT: Harry will be disappointed. Okay, we'll run over and see him.

LOGAN: He's at the Cassandra Club now. Just question him enough to make sure he thinks we're bearing down. God, I wish I could get my hands on him.

GRANT: You want him fixed for you, Sam?

LOGAN: I told you we got orders not to do anything.

GRANT: No, I mean so that it ain't our fault.

LOGAN: What do you mean?

GRANT: I could give Rudy a little call. He's burning up about March too. And we'd be in the clear.

LOGAN: Maybe that's an idea. But we've got to be in the clear.

GRANT: We will be. I'll take care of everything.

LOGAN: It'll make me sleep better. Thanks, Gene.

GRANT: It's a pleasure. Anything else, Sam?

LOGAN: Yeah. You'll probably be getting calls about any orders.

GRANT: Who'll call?

LOGAN: *He* will. You don't have to know his name in order to talk to him on the phone.

GRANT: Okay, okay. I only asked. I'll give your regards to March.

LOGAN: The only regard I got for that son of a bitch you couldn't give him in public. You just tell Rudy to be careful.

GRANT: Rudy's always careful. So long, Sam.

I'd just finished reading when the receptionist told me to go into the D.A.'s office. I tucked the sheets back in the manila envelope and walked in. Martin Yale was sitting behind his desk staring out the window. He looked around as I closed the door.

"Did you read them?" he asked.

"Yeah," I said.

"Let me have them, then," he said. He took the envelope and put it away in his desk. "Get anything out of it?"

"Not much," I said. "He's a careful boy, but then he wouldn't be where he is if he weren't careful."

"Where is he?" Yale asked quickly.

"At the top," I said. "If you thought I was using the expression because I knew who he was, you're wrong. I've got ideas, but this transcript didn't give them to me. You get anything from it?"

"No more than you," he said. "Of course, it would be nice

evidence against Logan and his two detectives—if we could use it."

"I thought you couldn't," I said.

"It would blow me right out of office," Yale said. "Ordinary wiretapping is bad enough, but tapping the wires of the city hospital … I gather from the fact that you're here that nothing much came of Grant's idea with Rudy."

"Not too much," I said. "I got a nighttime view of the hills, but the marines arrived before I got dizzy."

"The marines?"

"Yeah. In the person of Jan Lomer. I'd always thought he was a little fat to play hero roles, but he looked awful good last night."

"Lomer is smart," Yale said. "He's got a nose for the wrong kind of publicity."

I nodded. "He made me an offer, too."

"Oh? What kind?"

"A sacrifice play," I said. "He offered to wind the whole thing up for me, with the victim thrown in. He'd like me to take Logan. But if he doesn't look big enough to me, they'll give me the mayor of Aragon City."

Yale whistled. "They must feel that you're crowding them a little." He hesitated. "What are you going to do?"

"What do you think?"

"I'm not sure what I think," he said slowly. "You're bucking a lot of brass."

"Yeah," I said. "But there's nothing that melts any prettier than hot brass, and it's beginning to come to a boil. … You know, it's funny."

"Is it?"

"Yeah. It's funny because I haven't done a damn thing. If I'd gone yelling around town, or if I'd tried to throw the hooks into Grant and Fleming, or even Logan, the top layer would rest more easily. They'd know how to handle it. But because I haven't done anything, their collars are getting tight."

He nodded. "It's been a good policy so far," he said, "but it's beginning to get a little thin. Or had you noticed?"

"I've noticed," I said. "It means I've got to go to work. Maybe today. Anyway, not long after I call Lomer and tell him that I haven't lost any mayors."

The D.A. swiveled his chair around and stared out the window. "March," he finally said, "I agreed to work with the Civic Betterment Committee and let you appear as an investigator of this office. Since the Committee is made up of some pretty important people, politically, you might say that I did it because of that."

"I might," I said, "but I wouldn't. You did the wiretapping on your own before I asked, so your heart must have been in it somewhere."

"It is," he said. "I hate every bit of dirt in this town, March. I don't like the kind of wares that punks like Jan Lomer and Johnny Doll peddle. I don't like all the other things that spread out from crime like that. But there hasn't been much I can do about it. I can't buck a syndicate like that *and* the city police department *and* the city government from the mayor on down. I have a pretty good idea of almost everyone who is involved, but I can't buck them all. I don't have that kind of money. I don't have that kind of men working for me. And

I don't have that kind of political support from the people themselves."

"I know," I said. "Funny, isn't it, how it's the little guy in town—the guy who maybe bets two bucks on a horse now and then through a bookie, or slips a quarter once a week into a slot machine—who is really responsible for organized crime, but then he gets all upset when a guy like Kefauver tells him about it."

He nodded. "Another thing," he said. "I don't care much for Civic Betterment Committees. Most of them do nothing but make their members feel important. I like the Aragon City Committee even less. My personal opinion, completely off the record, is that Linn Willis, George Stern, Donald Reid, Dr. Jilton, or Sherman Marshall could singly or together be involved in the corruption of this city. There isn't a one of them that's any more honest than he has to be. Miss Russell isn't much better, but I doubt if she has the brains to be really involved. So I agreed to cooperate because of only one person on the Committee. Elizabeth Saxon is a rough-tongued, soured old maid, but they don't make them that honest anymore. And she wants to clean up Aragon City if it's the last thing she ever does."

"I know how you feel," I said, "but why give me the story of your life?"

He swung around to look at me. "Because you're stirring things up a little differently than anyone expected you would—with the possible exception of Miss Saxon. You know she was the one who insisted that you be hired?"

I nodded.

"Even I thought," he said, "that you might scurry around and turn up a few things. I thought you might even do such a good job as light a fire under a king-size guy like Sam Logan. But I'm beginning to think maybe I was wrong. I'd like to know how wrong."

"I'd like to know myself," I said.

"When I first thought I was wrong," he said, "I thought maybe you would dig up something on the top man and hand in a nice, polite report to the Committee. Then there'd be a dignified shuffle in town, a reform government would come in, but somewhere among the newcomers there'd be another guy with his hand out. Things would be under a new management, but it'd be the same old business."

"That's what Lomer is counting on," I said.

"He would be," Yale answered. He drummed on the desk. "But I can already see it isn't going to be like that. You want to know what I think now, March?"

"Sure."

"I think one of two things will happen—and will happen quick now. Either you'll be killed and there'll be a big stink with everyone pulling in their horns for a couple of months and we'll be right back where we were. Or you'll pull the pins out from under someone and there'll be a crash that'll make our earthquakes seem like nothing. If this happens and I'm ready, I can step in and do such a good broom job that hoodlums will break out in a rash every time they hear of Aragon City."

"I don't kill very easy," I said.

"Or," he went on, ignoring me, "you could still sell out.

Boys like Lomer and Doll can bring a lot of pressure and a lot of temptation."

"If I weren't a tired old man, I'd resent that," I said.

"Okay, so you won't sell," he said with a grin. "Where does that leave us?"

"What are you going to do if I pull some pins?" I asked.

"Everything else," he said. "Some of it's been ready for a long time. I've got a long list of officials in this city who I know are mixed up in it. Some of them I could have waded in and taken a long time ago. But they would have only been replaced. As long as the top man was around and I had nothing on him, there was no point to moving. But I've got a list. I've even got a list of phony names under which there are bank deposits and safety deposit boxes. If you can really pull any pins, I'm going to get me a whole flock of court orders and then sit and wait."

"I should have been a politician," I complained. "Then somebody else could do the dirty work while I sat and waited."

"You'd probably get bored," he said. He suddenly grinned boyishly. "Well, March, do I gamble on you?"

"Why not?" I asked. "The worst that can come up is a lemon—and you might hit the jackpot."

"What are you going to do?"

"How the hell do I know?" I asked. "I wish everybody would stop acting as if I were a mastermind. I'm just a guy trying to do a job. ... All I know is that everybody seems a little off balance, so I'm going to start pushing."

"When?"

"Right now."

"Okay," he said. "I'll start collecting court orders. I can always paper the apartment with them if worst comes to worst." He grinned at me and held out his hand. "Good luck, March. If you need any help, phone me."

"If I need any help," I said, "there won't be any telephone handy. And happy *nolle pros* to you, too."

I went out. Downstairs, I got in the Cadillac and drove across town to the old mansion I'd visited before. Since I'd already established a pattern of doing my spare talking to the old lady, I figured it was time to put it to really good use.

She was glad to see me. She was getting to look forward to my dropping by and tossing off a tidbit or two.

"Young man," she said when she came into the room where I was waiting, "did you run over Sam Logan?" I grinned. I'd been amused to notice that the D.A. had steered carefully away from any talk about the person or persons unknown who had run over Captain Logan. But not this old girl. She had to know everything.

"My car was stolen," I said.

"Don't give me evasive answers, young man," she said tartly. "Did you or didn't you?"

"Let's put it this way," I said. "I was the first person to know that Captain Logan was the victim of an accident. I'm thinking of starting a campaign to make Aragon City safe for pedestrians."

She beamed at me. "Young man," she said, "you don't know how much you've brightened up the life of an old lady."

"I like you, too," I said. "In fact, if you were only about forty years younger, I'd make a pass at you. In the meantime, how would you like to give me some help?"

"Doing what?" she wanted to know.

"Last night," I said, "the hospital telephone lines were tapped shortly after Captain Logan was admitted. And later he had a phone call from his boss—the Mr. X we're looking for."

"You found out who it was?" she asked breathlessly.

"Not exactly," I said. "But I think it may work out just as well. What I want you to do is call each member of your Committee and tell them that you've been talking to me. Tell them that I managed to overhear Logan's conversation with his boss and I expect to finish up the case by tomorrow. Then I want you to remember exactly what each of them says. Write it down if necessary."

"You think he'll give himself away?" she asked.

"Maybe not," I said. "But there may be something I can use in the answers. If nothing else, the phone call will spur someone into activity. When you've talked to all of them, call me at my apartment. I'll go right back there and wait."

She nodded eagerly.

"One more thing," I said severely. "You've been reading too many detective stories in your old age. So don't get any bright ideas about trying to get more information out of any of them. Even if you're sure. Just do what I told you and then relay it to me. Nothing more."

"Who are you giving orders to?" she demanded.

"To you," I said. "This is no detective story, old girl. These are all tough characters. So don't go sticking your neck out. Leave that to me. That's what you're paying me for."

"Pshaw," she said. "Are you telling me how to act? I know enough to keep my mouth shut once in a while." I wasn't sure that she did, but I hoped that I'd made the danger clear enough. I said good-bye and left.

I drove straight back to my apartment. It was eleven-thirty when I got there, but I was already hungry. I fixed myself some bacon and eggs. I was in the middle of my coffee when the phone rang. It was Betty.

"What are you doing?" she asked.

"Nothing," I said. "Remember, I told you that's the way I work. I'm just sitting around waiting for a telephone call from a woman."

"Me?" she asked.

"No," I said. "The one I'm waiting for is about seventy years old."

"Then I won't be jealous," she said. "But do you have to stay there and wait all afternoon?"

"Probably at least two or three hours," I said. "And after that I may be busy. Why?"

"I have the afternoon off," she said, "and I thought we might do something." She hesitated. "Maybe I could come up and see you until she calls. Or are you thinking again?" I knew I should say no, but I wanted to see her. And there shouldn't be any danger until after Miss Saxon had made the calls, maybe not until after I phoned Lomer. I weakened.

"Come ahead," I said. "I stopped thinking the minute you said that."

She laughed, and even the sound of it over the phone sent little shivers racing up my spine.

"I'll be right over," she said and hung up.

I finished my coffee and stacked the dishes in the sink. I had just walked back into the living room when the door buzzer sounded.

TEN

She stood in the doorway, looking at me. There was a softness in her face I had never seen there before. Her green eyes were soft and warm, like a summer ocean. She seemed to be breathing hard and fast, as though she'd come up the stairs too quickly, her breasts making sudden thrusts against the yellow silk of her blouse. I found myself breathing faster as though trying to match the rhythm.

She came through the door without a word. I closed the door and turned to look at her. She came into my arms with a little rush.

Her lips brushed across mine and it was like turning my lips up to the sun. They brushed again, lightly, then stayed there. I could feel her heart pounding against mine and I couldn't tell which was pounding the louder. Then she suddenly pushed me from her with an almost impatient gesture.

I went over and sat on the edge of the bed and watched.

It was like a dream, a dream that eliminated time and should never stop. She moved, slow and gracefully, across the room, the jacket slipping from her shoulders. She pulled it around and put it over the back of a chair. There was a whispered assent from a zipper and she stepped out of her skirt. Each button on her blouse surrendered its place slowly, then the yellow silk was draped over the brown suit. Her hands arched along her back and came away holding a wisp of white silk. She stepped out of her pumps and peeled the sheer stockings from each leg. Her hands moved like a ballet dancer's as they slid the white silk over her hips and down to where she could step from them.

She turned and looked at me, her eyes shy and proud. The feel of her beauty went through me sharply, like a shout of laughter, almost like pain.

She came across the room, her red hair tumbling over her ivory shoulders. Her eyes were clear and a deep-water green, until she looked like a beach nymph coming slowly up from the bottom of the ocean, setting each foot on a wave as she came nearer and nearer.

The waves came in slow and warm, with a steady power that thrust itself against the beach. And there was the pounding of the surf, like the pounding of two hearts.

And the waves came higher and higher, and faster and faster, until they covered the beach and the final wave, frosting whitely as it surged to the peak, broke over our heads and the surf beat in our ears.

Then the waves went stealing away, softly running back along the sand, ebbing into the depths, and there was only the warm sand and the sweetness of the air.

Then we were two again, and I lit two cigarettes and gave her one of them.

"I love you," she said sleepily.

"I love you," I answered. Then I looked at her in surprise. "What happened to the script?" I asked. "These lines weren't in it the last time I looked."

She laughed. It was a soft sound that made me reach over for her hand.

"I was ad-libbing," she said. "You can take your line back if you want to."

I thought it over. "No," I said. "It was a good line. I'll keep it in. But what happened? The last I knew, we were waiting for some kind of sign, or something."

"It came," she said simply. "Last night, when you vanished from the club. I knew it then. It suddenly seemed so simple and clear. That's why I had to see you today to tell you. I had to tell you. No matter what, I love you, Milo."

I leaned over and kissed her. "I know," I said. And the funny part was that I did know. "That's the way I feel too. Only I didn't know it last night. I didn't know it until you walked in here a few minutes ago."

She rolled over on her side and looked at me. "Were we good, Milo?" she asked.

"The best," I said. My voice shook just remembering. "Anything and everybody else has been highly overrated."

"Me, too," she said. "I never thought that before, Milo. It wasn't anything to wonder about. It was like a parlor game and one merely played it the best one could. But this wasn't playing, Milo. This was it. ... Am I a shameless hussy?"

"You're a delightful hussy," I said. "And I love you," I added. It wasn't a bit hard to say. I liked saying it, so I repeated it.

She put her head on my shoulder and we finished our cigarettes in silence.

She leaned over to crush her cigarette in the ashtray,

stretching her body like a cat. She glanced back and saw me watching her. She laughed, first with her eyes.

"I feel good," she said. "No matter what happens, Milo, I'm glad. You've made me feel clean and good for a minute. No matter what happens, that minute can't be taken away from me."

"We'll add to it," I said. "That's what will happen. We'll pour other minutes on it until it becomes hours and then we'll hoard hours—and days—and months—and years."

"I can almost believe it when you say it," she whispered.

Suddenly it had become that sort of day. There was nothing in the world but the two of us. And in the distance there was the murmur of the ocean and overhead there was the sun. There had never been a day like it before.

"Let's start it right now, Milo," she said. "Let's go now—somewhere—anywhere—and never look back or never think about what's behind. Let's go now while we have our hands on it."

That brought me back. Not all the way, but far enough to realize that I still had a job to do before I could do anything else. I sat up on the bed and looked down at her. As I looked, a tear rolled down her cheek. I leaned over to kiss away the one that followed it.

"What's the matter?" I asked. "Why are you crying?"

"Because I'm happy," she said. "And I'm afraid. I don't want to lose it, Milo."

"We won't lose it, honey," I said. "But I have to finish this job."

"I know you do," she said. "I was only wishing out loud,

Milo. I know that everything has to be done up in a nice, neat little parcel. But I can't help it if I'm afraid."

I didn't want her worrying, but it still made me feel good to think that she'd worry about me.

"It won't take long," I said. "I think maybe it'll be finished by tomorrow. Then we'll start living. Just you and me."

She rolled over on her stomach and reached to the small radio at the head of the bed. She found a station with music, turned the volume low. Then she rolled back to look at me.

"Tell me about it, Milo," she said softly.

So I told her about Denver, about where we'd live and what we'd do. I told her all about my work and about the hundreds of little things that gave me fun. I told her about the trips we'd take, all the things we'd do together. She lay there, with her eyes half closed, an expression on her face like a kid listening to the promises of Santa Claus.

"I can almost believe it while you're talking," she said dreamily when I'd finished.

"You can believe it, honey," I said. "It's all fixed. This one is strictly a boat race."

She nodded, that little smile still on her face. We sat there quietly, each of us building the dream in our hearts while the radio provided a love song.

The song came to an end and a voice said: "The two o'clock news, brought to you by the Froug Car Company*—the home of luxury cars at economy prices ..." The voice went on, giving the license numbers of radio specials, convincing the

* This name is probably one of the author's private jokes. William Froug was the name of the writer for the radio scripts based on the Green Lama character created by Ken Crossen.

listeners that a secondhand car was better than a new one, but I listened with only half my mind. I was still floating around on cloud number nine, and who cared about cars!

"Now to the news," the announcer said. "Federal narcotic agents today seized a cache of morphine and heroin, estimated at a value of two hundred and fifty thousand dollars, aboard a private yacht as it docked in Aragon City. It is believed the shipment was destined for a local crime syndicate. ... Aragon City firemen, answering an alarm on Third Street, broke into the house and discovered a double murder. Miss Elizabeth Saxon, sixty-eight-year-old native of Aragon City, and her seventy-five-year-old butler had both been shot to death. The time of death was fixed at about one o'clock by the coroner's office. Chief of Police Leo Gibbs has promised an early arrest ..."

The voice droned on but I didn't hear it. I felt like I'd been sandbagged over the head. I knew what had happened. She'd called the Committee members like I'd told her. And one of them had been more upset by the news than the others. The old lady hadn't been able to resist the temptation of probing a little deeper. I could almost see the expression on her face as she thought of being able to call me and give me a name instead of just reporting conversations. And she had probed too deeply. Someone had convinced her that he would come over to discuss it. Then he'd arrived, and the only conversation was in lead.

Me and my bright ideas about pushing them off balance. I'd used an old lady who had more guts than all the rest of the town put together, and now she was dead. She'd been lying there dead while I was sitting around with my eyes full of stars.

I didn't even realize the radio had been turned off, but I became aware that somebody was talking to me.

"Milo," Betty was saying, "I'm sorry ..."

"Sure, you're sorry," I said harshly. "Everybody will be sorry. They'll probably give her a lovely obit in the newspaper. But she's still dead. An old lady who only wanted to live in a clean town, a town she could be proud of—an old lady who never had any fun out of life and couldn't resist making just a little like a character in a book."

I checked the savagery in my voice and looked at her for the first time since I'd heard the news. Her face was white and drawn.

"I'm sorry, honey," I said. "I didn't mean to take it out on you. It's just that it's my fault that she was killed. And right now, I don't like myself so much."

"I understand," she said. Her eyes were tortured, as though she felt the pain that was inside of me. "I'm sorry." I got up and started putting on my clothes without paying much attention to them. "You'd better get dressed, honey," I said, "and go home. Things are going to start happening around here, and I don't want you in the line of fire."

She got up and dressed without saying a word. When she was finished, she turned to stare at me. Her green eyes were dark and troubled.

"It's been spoiled, hasn't it, Milo?" she asked. Her voice was hardly more than a whisper.

For a minute I came back to her. I put my arms around her and held her tight.

"Not spoiled, honey," I said. "It's just been sidetracked for the minute. I'm sorry, honey, but this is something I've got to clean up—I've got to scrub off all the spots—before I can live with you, myself, or anybody. I have to do a few things before there can be anything else."

"I understand, Milo," she said. "I guess I have to do a few things myself." She stretched up to kiss me. "Good-bye, Milo."

"Not good-bye," I said. "I'm too mad to get hurt. I'll be back. No later than tomorrow. Maybe tonight. Where will I find you?"

"I'll come back here," she said. "When I'm ready. I still have the key. I'd rather wait here—where there's some little part of you."

She turned and walked to the door. She opened it and looked back. "Remember that I love you, Milo," she said. "Remember that. It's the one real thing."

"I'll remember it," I said. I knew I could never forget it. "I'll remember it because you're going to be telling me every day after this."

She gave me a tight little smile and was gone. I closed the door and walked back into the room. Her scent was still there, but she was gone and the room seemed empty. But I felt empty inside too.

The phone rang. I picked up the receiver and said, "Yeah?"

"March, did you hear the news?" It was Martin Yale. His voice sounded tense.

"I heard the news," I said. "This is one you can mark up against me, Yale. This was March being the bright boy. I used her to point a finger and she didn't know it was loaded."

"It wasn't your fault," he said. "You didn't know it would backfire that way."

"It was my fault," I said. "I was mooning. I was caught in the oldest trap in the world. A trap that sets itself. When a man's planting a garden, he's got no business staring into the sun."

"What are you going to do now?" he asked.

"Light the candle at *both* ends," I said.

"What do you want me to do?" he asked. He didn't understand my remark, but he wasn't going to make an issue of it.

"Just stick around," I said. "Get yourself a good supply of court orders and a few wicker baskets. Keep the coroner's office alerted."

I hung up and stared at the phone. Finally I picked up the receiver and dialed Jan Lomer's number. It rang twice and then he was on the phone.

"Lomer," I said, "this is March."

"Ah, good afternoon, sir," he said. "I've been waiting for you to phone."

"Have you been listening to the news?" I asked him.

A note of caution crept into his voice. "I'm afraid not, sir. Have I missed something?"

"A friend of yours," I said evenly, "killed a friend of mine."

There was a long pause. "I'm afraid I don't understand," he said at last. "To the best of my knowledge, my more immediate friends have been completely inactive today."

"Not those friends," I said. "I mean a top man. A big, important man, a credit to his community and all that. He murdered an old lady. An old lady of whom I was becoming very fond."

"I'm sorry to hear that, Mr. March. I mean that, sir. I do not approve of such methods. Perhaps I'll have to make some new arrangements."

"Don't bother," I said. "I'll make them for you."

"Mr. March," he said heavily, "I trust you will not let sentiment interfere with business. This incident is most regrettable, but I'm sure that you and I can still work things out."

"Not anymore," I said. "I'm not buying and I'm not selling. From now on there's not going to be any neutral territory. I want to taste a little blood."

"I'm sorry to hear that, sir," he said. "You know what this means?"

"I know," I said.

"I like you, Mr. March. I don't like to take the step which this forces me to do."

"Go right ahead," I said. "It's going to be a long walk, so you might as well start now."

"Very well," he said. "Good-bye, sir."

I hung up and went into the kitchen. I got down the box of crackers and got out the old four-barreled gun. It felt good in the palm of my hand.

I went back into the living room, carrying a bottle of brandy and a glass with me, and sat down. I got a small can of oil from my suitcase and cleaned the gun carefully. Then I loaded it. I got out a special clip, a variation of the sort of spring clip which magicians use. It had been made to hold the small gun. I put the gun in it and fastened it to the inside bottom of my coat.

I stood up and pressed my arm flat against the side of my coat. The gun dropped into my fingers where they waited just below the edge of the coat. I tried it a few more times. Then I sat down to wait. I was as ready as I'd ever be.

They moved fast. I had to say that for them. It was maybe no more than twenty minutes later when the door buzzer sounded. It gave a short angry sound as though someone had impatiently jabbed a finger at the button.

I went to the door and opened it.

Harry Fleming stood there. His face was sleepy-looking but pleased, as though he were having a nice dream. There was a gun in his hand.

"This is it, sucker," he said. "Turn around." He gestured with the gun.

I turned around. He reached under my left arm and snaked my gun from its holster. He patted my pockets carefully.

"Okay," he said. "Turn back now."

I turned back. As I faced him, he slapped me across the cheek with the barrel of the gun. I felt the gun sight take a little skin with it. Some blood ran warmly down my jaw. But there was no pain in it.

"What is this?" I asked evenly. "An arrest?"

"Call it that if you like," he said. "Call it anything you want to. Come on."

I moved past him into the hallway. He closed the door and prodded me toward the stairs. We walked down in silence.

There was a sedan parked in front of the house. Fleming pushed me across the sidewalk and opened the back door. We got in. When we were inside I saw the driver was Rudy Cioppa. He was watching me in the rearview mirror as he started the car.

"Nice company you keep, Rudy," I said. "You keep running around with cops like this and the first thing you know you'll have a bad reputation."

Fleming rocked me with a backhand sweep of his left hand.

"Take it easy, Harry," Rudy said from the front seat. "The boss won't like it if we get blood all over the car." Harry said what the boss could do. His voice was thick. He was a little drunk, but not on liquor.

As we went around the corner, I got a glimpse of an MG pulling away from across the street. I could see the red hair blowing in the wind. She'd hung around and then seen me taken out. I cursed under my breath and hoped that she wasn't going to try to bring in the marines.

"Where are we going?" I asked as the big car picked up speed.

"A place," Rudy said. "We got a little unfinished business to take up with you, chum."

He turned another corner, heading toward the ocean. The motor roared as he stepped on the gas.

ELEVEN

We came to a stop in front of a huge building down on the oceanfront. It had once been a fancy beach club, but now it was empty and weather-beaten. There was still some flaked lettering across the front that said this was the Marisol Club.

"Isn't it a little early in the afternoon to start nightclubbing?" I asked.

"Not the kind we're going to do," Harry Fleming said. He liked it so much he repeated it, then laughed.

Rudy got out of the car and went over and unlocked the front door. Then Harry nudged me from the car and we crossed the sidewalk. There was plenty of traffic on the coast highway, but no one paid any attention to us. Across the street a fat lady, in a bathing suit that resembled one in name only, was putting money into a parking meter.

We went into the building and the door clicked shut behind us.

Inside, there was nothing of the club look left. It was like being in any old warehouse. About one half of the main floor was filled with boxes of various kind. Some of them were crates, holding slot machines. I could guess what was in the other boxes.

"Nice layout you got here," I said.

"It'll do," Rudy said. He grinned. "You know, everybody

feels real sorry for the guy that owns this building. They figure he's got a white elephant."

"Is the owner around?" I asked.

"Don't worry," Rudy said. "We'll take just as good care of you as if he was here himself."

"You're damn right we will," Harry Fleming said. He nudged me with the gun and we walked across the warehouse. Our footsteps echoed hollowly.

We went up a winding staircase to the second floor. There were several rooms there, and in some of them I could glimpse more crates and boxes. We turned in to one of the rooms, and it was fixed up with chairs and a desk. There was plenty of light in the room. I noticed the windows were covered with blackout curtains. I remembered that on the outside they were boarded up.

There was a man sitting at the desk. He looked up as we came in, staring at me.

It was Johnny Doll.

"Have any trouble?" he asked.

"Nah," Rudy said. "What trouble could we have? He's just one guy. He's been lucky up to now, but it's all run out now."

Johnny Doll nodded.

"Hello, Johnny," I said. "Somebody ought to tell you that it's considered more polite to send people invitations instead of always sending a guy with a gun. Somebody's liable to get the wrong impression of you."

"You're all through, March," he said. "They finally got around to listening to me. All this polite stuff sounds nice, but when the money's on the table, the only good cop is a dead cop."

"I'd agree with you if we were talking about Harry here," I said. "But in this case I'm a little prejudiced. But why bring me all the way over here to give me a fatherly talk?"

"This is a nice, safe place," Johnny Doll said. "There ain't much noise gets out of this place. Even if it should, there's too much traffic outside for anybody to know they're hearing gunshots. Then tonight there's a boat coming in to the beach here. When it leaves, it can take you along and dump you in the ocean."

"Neat," I said. "Not gaudy, but neat."

"Get it over with," Johnny Doll said, looking at Rudy. "We've got work to do."

Rudy Cioppa and Harry Fleming left my side and moved toward the desk. Then they turned to face me. Harry Fleming still had his gun in his hand. I felt a little naked standing there in the strong light while the three of them looked at me as if I were already dead.

"Me?" Harry Fleming asked. His voice was unsteady.

"Why not?" Johnny Doll said. There was a grin tugging at his lips, and I knew he liked the idea of having a cop do a job for him. "If it makes you happy, go ahead."

"But make it good," Rudy Cioppa said. He couldn't keep the contempt out of his voice. "The last time we let you shoot a guy, I had to finish him for you."

Harry Fleming cursed and started to raise his gun. I pressed my arm against my side and felt the little gun drop into my hand. It felt good.

I almost laughed when the first bullet hit Harry Fleming. He was still raising his gun when it hit him, and there was an instant for him to realize he'd never make it. His face set in a mask of surprise and disappointment—except for the spot on one cheekbone where the bullet smashed its way through.

I saw it all, but like a picture that's flashed before your eyes and then off, for I knew there was no time to enjoy it. Rudy Cioppa was already getting his gun out of his shoulder holster. There was no time for careful aiming. I just pointed the gun and pulled the trigger. I didn't even wait to see what happened, but swung back toward the desk. Johnny Doll was trying to go down behind the desk and get a gun out at the same time. He was trying to do too many things. I heard the third bullet hit and saw the first dark rush of the blood on his white shirt before he flopped out of sight.

There was another shot, and I looked down to see if I'd pulled the trigger again. I hadn't. Like a delayed signal, I felt the tug at my coat, the burn along my ribs after it had happened.

Rudy Cioppa was lying on the floor, the same set, dead expression on his face. He was propping his right hand up with his left, steadying the gun in it. A trickle of smoke came from the muzzle.

I leveled the small gun, but it wasn't necessary. Even as I tightened my finger, Rudy dropped his gun and slumped back.

The warehouse was quiet. Deadly quiet.

I stood there for a minute, looking at them. I didn't feel anything particularly, not even satisfaction. The tension was still with me, building up inside. I started to put the little gun in my coat pocket.

"Stand still, March," a voice said behind me. It was a voice filled with anger and hatred.

I stood still. There was a spot in my back that itched, like that was where a gun was pointing.

"Now turn around," the voice said. "Slowly."

I turned. Very slowly. Like I was standing on the point of a pin. I'd heard voices like that before.

A man stood in the doorway behind me. He held a gun in his hand, but not the way a professional holds one. He was an amateur, but that didn't mean anything except that he'd shoot even quicker. We stared at each other.

It was Linn Willis. The Chairman of the Aragon City Civic Betterment Committee. Owner of the Willis Aircraft Corporation. Owner of the *Aragon City News*. A man with a lot of money and a lot of power—but not enough of either.

He didn't look like *the* Linn Willis now. He didn't even look like the mysterious Mr. X, the power behind the throne. There was a rumpled look to him. His face was congested and twisted with hate. This was a man who found himself tearing down his own house.

"I had to come to see you die," he said, and his voice was strong with hate. It was no longer crisp, no longer the voice of a man who knew he would always be obeyed. "And it's good I did. It's better this way. I'll like it better. I'll kill you myself."

"Like you did Miss Saxon?" I asked softly.

"Yes," he said. "Yes, like I did her. It was easy. And it'll be easier with you. She was an old fool. I was against your being hired, but she had to have her way. And now look what you've done."

"I've been busy," I admitted. I was watching him closely. I knew he wasn't going to talk long.

He walked closer and I could see the whiteness of his knuckle over the trigger of the gun. I saw it start to whiten more and I shot through my pocket.

The bullet hit with a soft thud and I heard the breath hit in his throat. I reached out with my left hand and slapped the gun from his slack fingers.

He stood there for a minute, swaying only slightly. Maybe his hatred was keeping him on his feet. He didn't seem fully aware that he'd been hit. Then, like a man riding down an escalator, he slid below the level of my eyes, then folded to the floor.

I stood looking down at him. I could smell the scorched cloth of my coat and I could hear the breath fighting in his throat. A little froth of blood appeared between his clenched lips.

"That," I said, "was more for Miss Saxon than for all the other things you did. I hope she's watching from somewhere and knows that it's partly squared off now."

I don't think he heard me. His mouth was working as though he were trying to say something. There was death in his eyes, but that hatred was still keeping him alive.

"You—son of a bitch," he finally said. The words made the blood bubble between his lips. "You have to take everything from me, don't you? You have to have—everything—everybody—even—"

He died.

I went back to where Harry Fleming was lying and found

my regular gun in his coat pocket. I slipped it into my holster and walked back past the body of one of Aragon City's leading citizens. At the door, I turned for a last look at the room. There were four of them there, one for each barrel on my little clip gun, who would never again make a drug addict, put up slot machines for the school kids' lunch money, or take a cut from a sweaty prostitute.

I should have felt very good, but I didn't. I felt lousy.

I walked down the winding stairway and across the warehouse floor. I pushed open that front door and stepped out into the sun. I twisted my head around to look at it, shutting my lids against the glare. But just the warmth felt good. I heard a car drive away from the front of the building, but I didn't even bother to look up.

After a while I closed the door behind me. I walked down the street until I came to a cab stand. Then I took a cab back to Miramar Terrace. I didn't bother going up to the apartment. I climbed into the Cadillac and drove back across town. I stopped at the first drugstore and went in. I entered a phone booth and dialed the number where I knew a man was still waiting impatiently. I was so tired it was an effort to turn the dial on the phone.

He was on the phone almost as soon as I'd given my name to the girl.

"Well, March?" he asked. His voice was thin and tight.

"Okay," I said. My voice was so tired I hardly recognized it myself. "You can start using your court orders. And the wicker baskets."

"Who?" he asked.

"You know a big building down on the oceanfront?" I asked. "The one that used to be the Marisol Club?"

"Yes," he said.

"Well, get your boys down there fast. You'll find the place full of slot machines and drugs. And there's another load scheduled to come in sometime tonight. And on the second floor you'll find four dead men."

"Who are they?"

"Two hoodlums," I enumerated, "Johnny Doll and Rudy Cioppa. One Aragon City first-grade detective, Harry Fleming. One respectable citizen, Linn Willis."

"Linn Willis?" he said. "Are you sure, March?"

"I'm sure," I said. "Both that he's dead and that he was the guy we were looking for. I think you'll find that the gun beside him is the one that killed Miss Saxon."

"God!" he said.

"No," I said. "God wasn't around when Linn Willis was fashioned. He was a self-made man. Now he's unmade."

"My men are already on their way," he said. "What else?"

"That's about it," I said. "You already know where to find Captain Logan. The rest of it's on your little list. With Willis and Johnny Doll out of the way, the rest of them will fold fast. And maybe it's better this way. A court case on Willis might have been tough even with what you'll find."

"Uh-huh," he said. "What about Lomer?"

"I don't think you can get much on him," I said, "but I don't believe he'll bother you. The rest of it's up to you, Yale. I've planted your hangman's garden, but it's your harvest. You can do me one favor."

"What's that?" he asked.

"When you get around to it," I said, "call someone on what's left of the Civic Betterment Committee and tell them their chestnut is out of the fire. Tell them they can mail me my check at Denver. Or they can take it and stick it, for all I care."

"What are you going to do?"

"Catch the first plane back to Denver," I said.

"Well ..." he said, then hesitated a minute before going on: "You know, we will probably need you here later on for some testimony. You really shouldn't leave at all—with those four dead men down there."

"I know," I said, "but right now I don't like this city much. I'll get over it and I'll come back. You call me."

"Okay, March," he said. "It's not legal, but I'll clean it up for you."

"Thanks," I said. I hung up and went out to the car. I got in and drove over to the Canyon. I drove through the iron gates and up to the front door. I went up and rang the bell.

After a while the door opened and Jan Lomer stood in the doorway. He kept one hand back of the door and I knew what was in it, but I didn't care. He looked surprised, but not too surprised.

"Well, Mr. March," he said, "I didn't expect to see you here."

"I know," I said. "I owe you something, Lomer. I came to pay it to you. You've earned yourself a nice long vacation. Take it."

"They failed, eh?" he said. "All three of them?"

"Yeah," I said. "All three of them, and one more."

He looked at me with those old shrewd eyes. "Willis?" he asked finally.

"Willis," I said. "Aragon City ain't what it used to be. Right now, the D.A. is busy grabbing bank accounts and safety deposit boxes. But sooner or later he'll get around to you."

He nodded. "Why are you taking the trouble to warn me, sir?" he asked.

"I told you," I said. "I owe you for the other night when Rudy grabbed me before I was ready. Besides, what's the difference? You're an old man and you're through operating in America."

He just looked at me.

"The Combine," I said. "They won't like the way you've handled this."

"I'd thought of that, sir," he said. "In fact, Mr. March, it had already occurred to me that you might come out on top this afternoon. Men like Johnny Doll are all right in their way, but they don't stand a chance when they're up against a man with a cause. I have, sir, been packed ever since you phoned and told me about the regrettable death of your friend."

"Then I'm holding you up," I said. "So long. Don't take any wooden Cellinis." I turned toward my car.

"Mr. March," he called after me. I turned. "I think, sir, that I understand why you don't seem happier over your success. I'm sorry, sir."

"Go to hell," I said. I got in the car and drove back toward Miramar Terrace.

TWELVE

She was already in the apartment when I got there. Without a word, she came across the room and into my arms. I held her there for a moment, feeling the warmth of her body through my clothes, the scent of her filling my head with memories. Then I pushed her from me.

"I killed Linn Willis," I said.

"I guessed it," she said. Her voice was so low I could hardly hear it.

"He hated me," I said. "It was a special hate. And it was greater when he knew I'd killed him. He accused me of having to have everything and everybody. I thought about that as I walked down the stairs."

She said nothing.

"I've seen men before who hated me for destroying their dream world," I said. "But this was different. This was the hatred of a man for another man who's taken his woman. ... I came out of the building and someone drove away while the sun was in my eyes."

"You turned your eyes to the sun," she said.

"I know," I said. "Sometimes a man doesn't dare look at something he knows. I was remembering. Remembering the first time I asked you for a date and you said there was a call coming in on another line, then you came back and said you'd meet me. Remembering that there was no switchboard in the office, that there was only one phone."

She nodded.

"Remembering," I went on, "that the other night Linn Willis knew I was going to be at the Cassandra Club before I even got there—before I knew it myself. He knew I was going to be taken there. And he passed it along to Captain Logan, who passed it to Grant, who passed it to Rudy Cioppa."

"I wanted to tell you," she said, "but I couldn't until it was straightened out. I told you I had to do some things myself. Oh, for a minute, Milo, I wanted to just run away with you. But then I knew I'd have to straighten it out. I waited downstairs until I knew they were taking you. Then I went to him and told him that I loved you and asked him to let you go."

"So that's why he hated me so much," I said. "I could almost hate you for that myself. ... You had to make your report complete, didn't you?"

"No," she said and her voice was a thin cry. "No, Milo. I was trying to save you and make it a clean break."

"You reported everything," I said. It hurt, and I wanted to hurt back. "Did you also report this afternoon? Did you tell him how you kept me occupied while he was killing an old woman? Did you tell him how it was? Maybe you even made a little joke about it. Maybe you said, 'March came in like a lion and went out like a lamb.' Is that how it went?"

"Don't, Milo," she said. Her face was white and drawn, and her voice was like a knife in the night. "Don't. It was all real this afternoon. I loved you—I love you. I told you that no matter what happened, I would always love you. You said it, too, Milo. Don't you remember?"

I did remember. That was what hurt.

"It's not too late, Milo," she said. "This afternoon was important. Everything else is over with. Remember how you were telling me about Denver, about the life we'd have? We can still have it, Milo."

"No," I said. My voice sounded far away. "I'd never know, Betty. I'd always remember. Oh, not that you slept with him. But that you came to me because he wanted you to. That he was willing for you to come to me, maybe even willing for you to sleep with me as long as you didn't like it. I'd always remember that something made you go to a guy like that in the first place. You knew what he was. You must have wanted things—there must have been some hunger that drove you to him. I'd never know when you might get that again. I'd never be sure of anything."

She looked at me and the life went out of her eyes. They retreated and became just green spots in her white face. They looked the way I felt.

"All right, Milo," she said. "I had this afternoon and you can't take that away from me. I love you and that's still mine, too. I'm ready whenever you are."

"Ready for what?" I asked.

"Aren't you going to take me in?" she asked. "His money—the money he made from drugs, from slot machines, from whores—from other whores—paid for these clothes. I have more of that money in the bank. Aren't you going to arrest me?"

"No," I said. "I can't do that either, Betty. I can't go in and lay my heart on the D.A.'s desk and say, 'Here, put it in jail.' It's not that easy, Betty. ... It's got to go the way it is. This, right here and now, is your punishment—and mine too. It's remembering this day—all of it, from twelve o'clock right up to now. Never forgetting any part of it."

I turned and walked through the door without looking back.

Downstairs I got into the Cadillac. I drove south, past the city limits, through Ocean Park and Venice. Down Washington Boulevard, across Sepulveda and out to the International Airport. I left the Cadillac sitting in the parking lot and went inside. There was a seat on a plane leaving for Denver in five minutes. I bought a ticket and went out and boarded the plane.

When we were up over the city, I looked down and saw the lights. Somewhere among them was something called Aragon City. I looked down and tried to imagine that those tiny lights were all there was down there. But it didn't work. I could still remember.

ABOUT THE AUTHOR

Kendell Foster Crossen
(1910–1981), the only child
of Samuel Richard Cros-
sen and Clo Foster Cros-
sen, was born on a farm
outside Albany in Athens
County, Ohio—a village of
some 550 souls in the year
of this birth. His ancestors
on his mother's side include
the 19th-century songwriter
Stephen Collins Foster
("Oh! Susanna"); William
Allen, founder of Allentown, Pennsylvania; and Ebenezer
Foster, one of the Minute Men who sprang to arms at the
Lexington alarm in April 1775.

Ken went to Rio Grande College on a football scholarship
but stayed only one year. "When I was fairly young, I developed the disgusting habit of reading," says Milo March, and
it seems Ken Crossen, too, preferred self-education. He loved
literature and poetry; favorite authors included Christopher
Marlowe and Robert Service. He also enjoyed participant
sports and was a semi-pro fighter in the heavyweight class.

He became a practicing magician and had a passion for chess.

After college Ken wrote several one-act plays that were produced in a small Cleveland theater. He worked in steel mills and Fisher Body plants. Then he was employed as an insurance investigator, or "claims adjuster," in Cleveland. But he left the job and returned to the theater, now as a performer: a tumbling clown in the Tom Mix Circus; a comic and carnival barker for a tent show, and an actor in a medicine show.

In 1935, Ken hitchhiked to New York City with a typewriter under his arm, and found work with the WPA Writers' Project, covering cricket for the *New York City Guidebook*. In 1936, he was hired by the Munsey Publishing Company as associate editor of the popular *Detective Fiction Weekly*. The company asked him to come up with a character to compete with The Shadow, and thus was born a unique superhero of pulps, comic books, and radio—The Green Lama, an American mystic trained in Tibetan Buddhism.

Crossen sold his first story, "The Aaron Burr Murder Case," to *Detective Fiction Weekly* in September 1939, but says he didn't begin to make a living from writing till 1941. He tried his hand at publishing true crime magazines, comics, and a picture magazine, without great success, so he set out for Hollywood. From his typewriter flowed hundreds of stories, short novels for magazines, scripts radio, television, and film, nonfiction articles. He delved into science fiction in the 1950s, starting with "Restricted Clientele" (February 1951). His dystopian novels *Year of Consent* and *The Rest Must Die* also appeared in this decade.

In the course of his career Ken Crossen acquired six pseudonyms: Richard Foster, Bennett Barlay, Kent Richards, Clay Richards, Christopher Monig, and M.E. Chaber. The variety was necessary because different publishers wanted to reserve specific bylines for their own publications. Ken based "M.E. Chaber" on the Hebrew word for "author," *mechaber.*

In the early '50s, as M.E. Chaber, Crossen began to write a series of full-length mystery/espionage novels featuring Milo March, an insurance investigator. The first, *Hangman's Harvest,* was published in 1952. In all, there are twenty-two Milo March novels. One, *The Man Inside,* was made into a British film starring Jack Palance.

Most of Ken's characters were private detectives, and Milo was the most popular. Paperback Library reissued twenty-five Crossen titles in 1970–1971, with covers by Robert McGinnis. Twenty were Milo March novels, four featured an insurance investigator named Brian Brett, and one was about CIA agent Kim Locke.

Crossen excelled at producing well-plotted entertainment with fast-moving action. His research skills were a strong asset, back when research meant long hours searching library microfilms and poring over street maps and hotel floorplans. His imagination took him to many international hot spots, although he himself never traveled abroad. Like Milo March, he hated flying ("When you've seen one cloud, you've seen them all").

Ken Crossen was married four times. With his first wife he had three children (Stephen, Karen, Kendra) and with his second a son (David). He lived in New York, Florida, Southern California, Nevada, and other parts of the country. Milo

March moves from Denver to New York City after five books of the series, with an apartment on Perry Street in Greenwich Village; that's where Ken lived, too. His and Milo's favorite watering hole was the Blue Mill Tavern, a short walk from the apartment.

Ken Crossen was a combination of many of the traits of his different male characters: tough, adventuresome, with a taste for gin and shapely women. But perhaps the best observation was made in an obituary written by sci-fi writer Avram Davidson, who described Ken as a fundamentally gentle person who had been buffeted by many winds.

Made in the USA
Middletown, DE
19 July 2020